Conan the Cimmerian
Red Nails

The Screenplay

A complete adaptation of the classic story
by Robert E. Howard

Oscar Cintronmarina

Conan the Cimmerian
Red Nails

The Screenplay

Psalm 91:2, Douay

"It is good to give praise to the Lord:
and to sing to thy name, O most High"

In memory of Robert E. Howard

WHITE SCREEN

SUPER:

        "CONAN THE CIMMERIAN"

        "RED NAILS"

The letters for "Red Nails" begin to bleed and as the blood
pools at the bottom, it rises until the screen is completely
covered in a ghastly red.

FADE IN:

EXT. FOREST - POOL - LATE AFTERNOON

From a small pool hedged in by immense trees, the shadowy
figure of a horse's head reflects from the surface of the dim
water hole. The rider is indistinguishable.

The horse finishes slaking its thirst and its golden,
tasseled bridle is gently pulled by braided, leather reins
and its flanks are tapped likewise by soft leather, wide-
topped boots in silver stirrups, reaching up just below the
rider's bare knees.

EXT. FOREST - LATE AFTERNOON

The worn-out horse is driven further into the gloomy forest
and some distance from the pool, the rider stops.

The horse struggles to remain standing, its legs spread wide
apart and its head hangs low to the ground with labored
breathing.

VALERIA, 28, rises on one of the silver stirrups, dismounts
and ties off her mount to a small tree.

Valeria, a tall and curvaceous woman, turns and confronts a
vast, dismal and disquieting ancient forest.

Though splendidly figured, her frame hints at uncommon
strength, yet her beauty and femininity cannot be hid.

Her golden, curly tresses are cut square down to her
shoulders and kept in place by a satin red headband.

Her impressive, shapely breasts are covered by a low-cut,
wide-collared silk shirt with wide long sleeves exposing a
generous amount of her milk-white cleavage.

Girdled around her small waist is a wide silken sash that
holds up her wide-leg, silk breeches that end several inches
above the knees.

Attached to her rounded hips are a straight two-edged sword
and a dagger and with her hands resting on their pommels, she
looks up with wide ocean-blue eyes into the canopy of
interlocking branches blocking out much of the sunlight.

A slight, involuntary shudder surges through her firm
shoulders as she scowls and levels out her eyes.

> VALERIA
> Damn this blasted forest!

She heads east and occasionally glances back towards the pool
and her stallion to solidify her bearings.

A deathly silence reigns throughout the dreary forest. The
sounds of insects, birds and mammals are eerily absent. Not
even her movements can break the spell.

Ahead, she discerns an outcropping that leads to a steep and
high crag with its summit hidden from her view by the leaves
of the branches surrounding it.

EXT. FOREST - CRAG - LATE AFTERNOON

Up the steep crag she climbs following the ridge-like ramp
leading towards the top and after being buffeted by the
branches and leaves encircling the crag, the blazing sun,
hanging between sky and horizon, floods the top of her
wondrous, golden head with much welcomed sunlight.

Atop she finds footing on a level and spacious summit.

At fifty-feet up, the summit of the crag is about flush with
the treetops and on its eastern edge rises a horn-like
projection, angled outwards -- the pinnacle of the crag.

The forest top stretches out before her like an endless
emerald plateau.

Her restless eyes discover a bit of white beneath the layers
of accumulated leaves. She brushes the leaves aside with a
booted, shapely leg to find a human skeleton.

She studies it, unperturbed, accustomed to such sights.

She kneels beside it and scrutinizes the bleached bones from
one end to the other, mystified. The skeleton appears
complete -- not a single bone is missing or broken.

Valeria glances at the pinnacle, stands up and scurries up the horn-like projection and holding onto the peak, casts her eyes towards the northern horizon.

From her commanding view, the impenetrable canopy below her spreads like a great green undulating blanket as far as the eye can see with a vague hint of hill country at the horizon.

She then takes a gander at the eastern and western horizons with the same results minus the suggestion of hills.

Valeria faces the southern horizon and shielding her eyes with one hand, she discerns the forest becoming sparse and ebbing a mile out and then suddenly ending altogether to become a plain littered with cacti.

Valeria's bewildered eyes spot something else. She sucks in her breath in astonishment.

Miles out from where the forest ends, a great walled, oval-shaped city stands out on the plain filled with towers, turrets, and spires rising high above the ramparts and parapets.

The strain of hanging onto the pinnacle takes its toll and Valeria drops down to the crag proper.

A subtle sound of leaves being disturbed wheels her around like a tigress. Instantly her sword arm crosses over and latches onto the sword's grip at her left hip.

                    VALERIA
          Conan!

CONAN, 30, stands before the surprised, but beautiful pirate, grinning with his large, heavy arms crossed and resting on his massive chest.

At seven-foot tall, he's a clean-cut mountain of muscles rolling symmetrically beneath his dark bronzed skin. His outfit mirrors Valeria's except for the broad leather belt supporting a broadsword and poniard, instead.

His smouldering blue-eyes devour the girl's magnificent figure, his gaze lingering on her marvelous, prominent bosom.

Valeria releases the sword grip and drops her hand on a fine rounded hip. She does not mistake the fire in his eyes, yet being a woman...

                    VALERIA
          What are you doing here?

Still grinning.

                    CONAN
          You know very well why I'm here.
          Did I not praise your charms at
          every opportunity? Did I not
          express my esteem for you from the
          moment we met?

She nods with a sneer on her lips.

                    VALERIA
          Yes, I remember... you were as
          subtle as a bull. Did you trail me
          or did the others finally run you
          out on your ear from Zarallo's
          camp?

Conan erupts in laughter at her brazenness.

                    CONAN
               (grins; flexes arms)
          That whole lot of those dogs is no
          match for me -- of course I trailed
          you! And you should be thankful
          that I did, wench.

Conan answers Valeria's questioning eyes.

                    CONAN
          After you ran that Stygian officer
          through, the Stygians branded you a
          renegade and not even Zarallo can
          protect you now.

Valeria breaks eye contact with Conan and staring at the
ground shakes her fine banded head bitterly.

                    VALERIA
               (looks at Conan)
          What else could I to do? You heard
          how he provoked me, did you not?

Conan nods.

                    CONAN
          He deserved it. I wish I could
          have been there... I would have
          split his skull open like a melon.
          But what did you expect among
          soldiers and mercenaries?

Valeria kicks the ground scattering leaves.

                         VALERIA
              Argh! Why can't they see me as a
              man?

                         CONAN
                    (grinning)
              Do you have to ask?!

Conan's thirsty eyes go over every line of her ravishing
body.

                         VALERIA
              What are you grinning about?

                         CONAN
              The idea that you could ever be
              seen as a man, much less treated as
              one.

                         VALERIA
              Well, wipe it off. I don't like
              it.

Conan shrugs off her scratching claws.

                         CONAN
              You were right to leave, though.
              Those Stygians would have cut your
              heart out. And something else...
              did you know his brother was on
              your trail, and closing fast?

Valeria's quick eyes flash at the news and lock with Conan's,
who raises an eyebrow and nods, a grim smile playing on his
thin lips.

                         CONAN
              I didn't think so. If I hadn't
              closed with him, he would have slit
              your pretty throat from ear-to-
              ear... and I wouldn't have liked
              that.

She overlooks his last comment and motions impatiently with a
hand.

                         VALERIA
              And, what happened?

                         CONAN
              What?

                         VALERIA
              To the Stygian.

                    CONAN
               (annoyed)
          What do you think happened... I
          left his headless corpse to rot in
          the sun and because of it I almost
          lost your trail. Otherwise, I
          would have found you long ago.

                    VALERIA
          I'm not going back.

                    CONAN
          You don't have to -- and stop being
          such a harpy. You know very well
          I'm not like the officer you ran
          through... though with him and his
          brother out of the way, it would be
          easier, but it wouldn't be wise.
          The Stygians have a long memory.

                    VALERIA
          If not Zarallo's camp, what then?

                    CONAN
          You and I could --

                    VALERIA
          -- You and I? As in we? Ha! I'd
          rather go back and face the
          Stygians, than be seen with the
          likes of you... a penniless
          barbarian.

                    CONAN
          Your hollow taunts don't fool me.
          I've captained larger ships and
          crews than you ever did with the
          Brotherhood... and thrown away
          enough gold throughout the ports of
          the world, to fill a ship's entire
          cargo hold.
               (laughs)
          And as for money, you're just as
          impoverished as I am -- and don't
          try to deny it by playing high
          horse. But what does it matter?
          What pirate or mercenary isn't
          coinless, at one time or other?

Valeria leans back against the crag's peak, hands resting on
her curves, and regards Conan with a mocking stare and a hint
of humor on her lovely lips.

                    VALERIA
          Tell me, my bold and erstwhile
          captain... where are these myriad
          of ships and hosts of men, hmm?

Conan sees through her mask of scorn and grins in esteem at
her demeanor.

                    CONAN
          In the ocean's belly, mostly. My
          last ship was sunk off the coast of
          Shem by a Zingaran warship...
          that's why you found me with
          Zarallo's Free Companions.

Conan moves closer to her -- a towering Cimmerian before a
blonde bombshell.

                    CONAN
          But I soon regretted it once we
          arrived at the frontiers of Darfar.
          Beggarly pay and wine to boot --
          and I had no taste for the black
          women that came to the camp at
          Sukhmet... filed teeth and rings
          through their noses. Cannibals,
          the whole lot of them!

Conan's eyes look deep into Valeria's, who doesn't shy away.

                    CONAN
          Now, you. What forced you off the
          decks and into Zarallo's nest of
          cutthroats?

Valeria glares at him and then looks away.

                    VALERIA
               (cross)
          Red Ortho! The bastard wanted to
          make me his concubine. So during
          the night, while the ship lay
          anchored off the Kushite coast, I
          jumped overboard and swam to the
          shores of Zabhela.

Uncomfortable with Conan's close proximity, she moves away
from him as she continues her tale, creating more space
between herself and the Cimmerian.

                    VALERIA
        The next day I learned from a
        Shemite merchant that Zarallo and
        his men were guarding the Stygian
        frontiers from Darfar incursions.
        I needed money, so that same day I
        joined an eastern caravan to
        Sukhmet... the rest you know.

Conan shakes his thick black, square-cut mane.

                    CONAN
        You were reckless to flee southward
        as you did... but fortunate
        nonetheless that you did so.
        Zarallo's men and the Stygians
        never considered taking this route
        in their search for you and only by
        sheer luck, did the man's brother
        happen upon your trail.

Valeria subconsciously begins to twirl one of her golden
locks.

                    VALERIA
        What have you in mind to do... now
        that you've found me?

Conan considers her with his dark, scarred countenance, his
moody eyes trying to penetrate the veneer of her words.

                    CONAN
        Head west towards the open country
        where the black tribes herd cattle.
        I've plenty of friends there. And
        from there to the coast, where you
        and I shouldn't have any trouble
        finding a ship. I've had my fill
        of these endless tracks of forests.

Valeria gives him a right to the jaw.

                    VALERIA
        Good, then move along... I have
        other plans.

                    CONAN
        Come to your senses, woman! It's
        madness to push on through this
        forest.

                    VALERIA
        I can and I will.

                         CONAN
              To what end?

                         VALERIA
              Since when are you my lord and
              master? My business is my own!

In level tones Conan tries to make her see otherwise.

                         CONAN
              Think you that I followed you all
              this way only to return with
              nothing to show for my time and
              effort? Cease this wasteful
              bickering, wench... you'll be safer
              with me, anyhow, than going it
              alone.

Conan takes a sudden reckless step towards her and Valeria
leaps back like a vicious leopard, her straight two-edged
sword flashing in her hand.

                         VALERIA
              One more step, Cimmerian dog, and
              I'll ram this sword through your
              gullet!

Conan stops dead in his tracks, the point of her sword
swaying menacingly before him, like a cobra.

                         CONAN
              Don't force me to take that
              plaything from you and throw you
              over my knee.

A mocking mirth spreads across her beautiful face as she
goads the Cimmerian onward, her ocean-blue eyes ablaze.

                         VALERIA
              An empty boast! Unarmed, no man
              can take this sword away from me.

Conan's eyes gleam at the taunting beauty before him. Her
white skin and flowing golden hair tempting him into a rash
embrace.

Conan scowls at Valeria, tormented, just shy of his desire!
A gleaming sword point between him and her ample bosom.

                         CONAN
              You teasing, wench! I'll peel your
              hide if it's the --

He moves towards her and Valeria coils her blade for a deadly thrust when suddenly they're both jolted by the horrendous NEIGHING and SCREAMING of their terrified horses, interrupting the touchy tableau.

Conan wheels about with the alacrity of a panther, his huge broadsword in his hand.

Both of them stand side-by-side alert and primed for action.

>   VALERIA
>   (shaken)
>   By Mitra, that does not sound good.

Conan shakes his head slowly in full agreement keeping his faculties focused on the havoc being wrought below.

The agonizing screams of their mounts heighten, mingled with the snapping and splintering of bones.

She glances up at him seeking answers.

>   VALERIA
>   Lions?

Conan shakes his head again.

>   CONAN
>   Not likely. Did you hear a roar?

Valeria shakes her head, now more puzzled than before.

>   CONAN
>   Neither did I. Listen to those
>   bones break! Lions don't kill that
>   way -- nor can they!

With Valeria in tow, Conan quickly but silently descends the ridge-like ramp from the crag top through the clutter of branches and leaves.

>   CONAN
>   (whispering)
>   Unfortunately, I tied my horse next
>   to yours, but how was I to know?

The frenzied, fear-laden sounds of their mounts cease once they're past the enveloping branches surrounding the summit of the crag.

>   CONAN
>   Stay lively.

From their height advantage they find themselves immersed in
the green-tinted gloom of the forest. Giant stalwart trees
stand around and about them and the ones further in the
distance seem more like vague spectres, shape-shifting in the
murky shadows.

The meager light straying in beneath the massive canopy above
them, reaches the duff only to cast a sparse, spellbinding
and eerie ambience that pervades throughout.

>   CONAN
>   (whispers)
>   They should be just past those
>   thickets.

Beyond the thickets the sickening sound of flesh being torn
and ripped apart and the snapping and crunching of bones
affects Valeria's innate feminine nature as she instinctively
and unconsciously lays a white hand on his powerful bronzed
arm.

>   CONAN
>   Definitely, not lions. They don't
>   make that kind of noise when they
>   feed. Whatever it is, it's big.

As soon as the words leave his mouth, a strong breeze catches
them from behind and heads towards the unknown creature.

Conan, realizing the significance of the tell-tale wind,
swears under his breath.

>   CONAN
>   Crom!

Suddenly, the horrible feast stops abruptly.

>   CONAN
>   Get ready, it's coming this way!

The high thickets shake uncontrollably as if in a great
quaking convulsion and Valeria, wide-eyed, takes a strong
grip around the Cimmerian's large arm.

>   CONAN
>   (amazed)
>   The thing must be huge! What the
>   hell --

A gigantic monstrosity from the past, pokes its humongous
head out from the thick, tall brush. Rows of yellowed, large
pointed teeth fill it's gapping, grinning jaws surrounded by
blood-covered, pendulous lips.

Its reptilian nose crunches into a wrinkled mess as it samples the air, its enormous maw dripping fresh spilled blood, with its huge dead staring eyes glued to the two adventurers high up along the side of the crag.

A long neck with serrated spikes slowly elevates the head and then it charges!

>   CONAN
>   Quick! Back up the crag! It can't
>   climb but it can rear on its hind
>   legs.

Moving backwards, Conan pulls Valeria behind him as he keeps his eyes fixed on the gigantic nightmare.

Its immense, barrel-shaped body with a high serrated spine -- that not even Conan could reach -- tramples down trees and brush as it plows through the forest towards them on short pudgy legs, with its white belly nearly scraping the ground followed by a long, spiked tail.

Valeria and Conan race through the barrier ring of branches and foliage and Valeria daring to look back sees the colossal creature rear up on its enormous rear legs, and panics.

Valeria freezes, dumbfounded as its snout reaches into the heights of the trees.

Coming up rapidly from behind, Conan grabs her wrist and jerks her upward through the clutter of branches and leaves up to the top of the crag, and suddenly the sun is in her eyes.

Just as they find their footing upon the safety of the crag's summit, the rearing relic of the past lands on the side of the crag with its forelegs and shakes the rock to its foundations.

The creature's head crashes through the barrier of branches and leaves, to drop its wide-open, cavernous jaws on the outer lip of the crag's summit, scattering leaves every which way -- its dead, dreadful and unblinking eyes watching them as if through time and space.

>   CONAN
>   You'd think two horses would be
>   enough -- but it's a greedy
>   devil... look at it.

The giant jaws, swiftly snap through empty air colliding together with a powerful metallic-like force.

It then yanks its mega-head downwards and disappears.

Conan and Valeria ease over to the edge to peek down through the carnage of broken branches and crushed foliage, towards the creature, to find it sitting on its haunches, like a colossal canine, looking up towards them as if waiting to be thrown a morsel.

Valeria's shoulders shudder.

> VALERIA
> Well, it can't stay there forever.
> It's bound to leave sooner or
> later.

Valeria's eyes follow Conan as he strolls over to the skeleton, crouches next to it, taps it on the skull with his knuckle, and glances at her.

> CONAN
> He probably thought the same thing.

Conan takes a moment to study the remains.

> CONAN
> No broken bones... he must have
> starved to death waiting for that
> hellhound to leave -- or another
> like it.

Conan, cool and untroubled by their predicament, sits down on an outcropping rock shaped like a square tree stump alongside the pinnacle.

> CONAN
> In their legends, the blacks
> mention such a a creature... a
> dragon. And if it is, it will
> never leave... not until we're
> dead.

Valeria stares at Conan, mortified as she struggles to quell a surging panic within her and unconsciously she moves towards Conan, drawn to his fearless nature and barbaric strength.

> VALERIA
> It's got to eat and drink, doesn't
> it?

> CONAN
> The pool is nearby and he just
> finished off our horses... and this
> dragon, as I suspect it is, is like
> a snake...
> (MORE)

>   CONAN (CONT'D)
>   it can live a long time without
>   food and water -- but unlike a
>   snake it doesn't need to sleep it
>   off after a large meal.

A sudden, desperate thought crosses her mind.

>   VALERIA
>   The trees! We could travel high
>   above it through the trees.

>   CONAN
>   It won't work. The branches around
>   this rock won't hold our weight --
>   and what's worse, I don't think
>   there's a tree it can't knock down.

Valeria's temper flares.

>   VALERIA
>   Are we to sit here then, on our
>   breeches, until we end up like
>   that?! Not I!

Valeria kicks the skull across the crag's shelf rustling up
the leaves.

Her eyes light up like wildfires.

>   VALERIA
>   I won't stand for it! I'd rather
>   shove my sword in its throat than
>   wait for death.

Conan watches Valeria with an appreciative eye in her wild
abandon -- her beautiful figure trembling with fighting
spirit -- but he does not voice it.

>   CONAN
>   Come here...

Conan surprises Valeria by taking her by the hand and pulling
her down onto his knee.

>   CONAN
>   ... And sit, and don't be so
>   anxious to get yourself killed.

Valeria, taken off-guard, doesn't resist as Conan takes her
sword and slides it back into its sheath.

>   CONAN
>   Your sword is no match for its
>   thick scales, anyway.
>   (MORE)

                    CONAN (CONT'D)
          It would only bounce off its armor
          and then he'd swallow you whole or
          squash you underfoot. Alive, we'll
          get out of this mess -- but not
          dead.

Quiet fear assails Valeria of the Red Brotherhood but,
comforted by his strength and confidence, she sits docilely
on his lap with Conan's arm snug around her small waist while
with his other hand, he fondles her thick, curly locks.

Meanwhile, Valeria's restless eyes discover large dark-red,
rounded fruit hanging from the higher branches of a tree with
striking, lucid leaves unlike the others surrounding them.

                    VALERIA
               (points)
          Look, there's fruit! We won't go
          hungry after all. It's both food
          and water.

Conan follows the direction of her finger.

                    CONAN
          We might as well throw ourselves to
          the dragon, rather than eat that.
          They're known as Derketa's Apples,
          by the blacks of Kush. Just a drop
          of its juice in your mouth or on
          your skin, and you'll be dead
          before you take a single step.
          Derketa, is the Queen of the Dead.

Valeria's hope is crushed.

                    VALERIA
               (crestfallen)
          That deadly? Are you certain?

Conan nods and Valeria falls into a dispirited silence.

Calm and seemingly oblivious to their entrapment, Conan's
focus is elsewhere -- his hands take stock of her waistline
and golden tresses.

Valeria regards him for a few moments.

                    VALERIA
          Why don't you give your hands a
          rest and climb up that horn.
          There's something you need to see.

Conan meets her beautiful eyes, shrugs his huge shoulders and
climbs up the peak.

He searches the horizons. Suddenly his eyes squint and he throws a hand over his wide brow as his eyes spy far into the distance, the walled city.

Conan's giant frame clings to the top in heroic fashion, motionless as a bronze statue.

> CONAN
> A walled city, no less -- so that's
> where you were going when you tried
> to get rid of me.

> VALERIA
> That's not why -- In fact, I
> discovered it right before you
> arrived... I just prefer traveling
> alone.

Conan, focused on the great walled city, doesn't seem to hear Valeria.

> CONAN
> I never thought to find a city in
> this forsaken land. The blacks
> don't build cities like that and
> the Stygians don't venture this far
> east -- it seems dead... no cattle,
> no crops... no people.

> VALERIA
> You can see all that from up there?

Conan nods and drops back down to the crag floor.

> CONAN
> Even if people are living there,
> they're too far away to do us any
> good -- and even if they could,
> they probably wouldn't... the
> blacks are not a friendly people,
> especially to foreigners and
> mercenaries like us. They'd rather
> shove their spears into us ra --

Conan's face is struck by a sudden inspiration, as his eyes fall upon the red round fruits mixed among the leaves.

> CONAN
> (thinking aloud)
> Blast me for a fool! Spears!
> That's it! I can't believe I
> didn't think of it before. Serves
> me right for allowing myself to get
> bewitched by a beautiful woman.

Conan looks her over, a slight smile on his lips

                    CONAN
          I can't think straight when I'm
          around you.

                    VALERIA
          Spears? Bewitched? Make sense,
          will you.

Conan ignores her and glides down the ramp until he's among
the branches surrounding the crag.

Looking through the foliage, he sees the dragon still sitting
on its haunches looking up towards the crag with the patience
of eternity.

                    CONAN
               (mutters)
          You foul waste of flesh.

Deftly and quickly, Conan begins cutting down long and thin
straight branches.

The noise stirs the ponderous creature into movement, it's
spiked tail lashing from side to side.

Conan, with a wary eye on the beast, finishes with the third
and last branch and starts cutting off vines.

Before the dragon can get worked up for another assault upon
the crag, Conan hurries back up to the crag shelf with the
branches and vines.

Valeria's confused face stares at the Cimmerian.

Conan motions with his head towards the engulfing branches.

                    CONAN
          They're too weak for us to climb
          through, but there's strength in
          numbers.

He begins to strap together the three branches, which are an
inch in diameter and about seven feet long, using the vines.

                    CONAN
          The Aquilonian rogues who would
          come to our country to recruit men,
          to fight against their own
          countrymen, would always say to
          us... "there's strength in
          numbers." But we Cimmerians prefer
          to fight as clans.

Valeria, exasperated, glares at Conan as if he's lost his mind.

>   VALERIA
>   What in a shark's eye has that to
>   do with branches and vines?

Conan grins.

>   CONAN
>   You'll see.

LATER

Conan, finishing tying the branches together, pulls out his poniard and forces the handle into one end of the joined shafts and secures the blade in place using more vines.

Conan stands the finished, rugged spear on its butt, now surpassing his height.

Valeria, arms across her chest, is unimpressed.

>   VALERIA
>   What? You plan to tickle it to
>   death? Didn't you say its armor
>   was --

>   CONAN
>   -- It's not completely covered in
>   scales. There's always another
>   way. If you look, you'll always
>   find a chink in any armor.

With spear in hand Conan descends down into the branches and leaves and then very carefully he thrusts the poniard upwards into one of Derketa's Apples.

A purplish-red juice drips from the pierced fruit. Slowly, he pulls out the blade smeared in its deadly toxin. He moves back up, keeping the blade as far away from himself as possible and shows it to Valeria, the blade now covered in a purplish tint.

>   CONAN
>   There's enough poison on that blade
>   to kill ten elephants, but that
>   thing may be immune to it -- I
>   don't know. We'll just have to try
>   and see.

Conan, with Valeria at this side, looks down through the broken branches straight at the crouched dragon.

                         CONAN
                 What are you looking at, you
                 miserable pig-dog!

The dragon blinks. Once. Twice.

                         CONAN
                 What's the matter? Are you afraid
                 to come up here, you son of a
                 thousand whores!

Valeria looks at Conan with a raised eyebrow at his colorful
invectives.

The dragon begins to stir -- it's evil eyes glaring at its
verbal tormentor.

                         CONAN
                 Come up here you fat, dung-faced
                 coward -- or do I have to come down
                 there and smash you into the earth
                 with my fists!

The

DRAGON

goaded by Conan's taunts throws its huge bulk suddenly upward
into the air.

CONAN

takes a few quick steps backwards bumping into Valeria and
forcing her back as well.

The gargantuan

HEAD

lands with a tremendous thud on the outer lip of the crag and
the creature opens its maul and emits a deafening bellow that
vibrates not only the air around them but the rock itself.

CONAN

darts forward and shoves the poison-smeared poniard -- hilt
deep -- into the red inner corner of the screaming dragon's
jaw.

Instantly its

JAWS

chomp down on the spear, severing the shafts and jerking
Conan forward but

VALERIA

grabs hold of his sword belt in the nick of time and stops
his forward fall into the creature's insatiable jaws.

CONAN

glances back at her with a grateful grin. The

DRAGON

retracts its head with the remaining portion of the spear
still embedded in its mouth and

CONAN

tosses aside the severed spear shaft.

EXT. FOREST - LATE AFTERNOON

The dragon, in a fit of frenzy, shakes its head wildly while
opening and closing its massive jaws in a frantic attempt to
dislodge the man-made thorn.

It snorts, coughs, and gags and then shoves its snout and one
side of its head into the ground and then spins around it a
few turns like a compass -- its rump high in the air.

Just as suddenly it stops and, rising up, paws its head. It
then opens its mouth to its widest extent and with its wicked
claws tries to rip out the remaining shaft and blade, and
after a few attempts, rakes out the thorn in its mouth.

Slowly it raises its head to look up, its human-like eyes
concentrated on his tormentors as blood drips from one side
of its jaw.

The copper brown scales on its back and sides become a
flaming, crimson red.

It then fills the forest with terrible, unworldly bellowing,
screams and roars.

EXT. FOREST - CRAG - LATE AFTERNOON

Valeria is visibly shaken by the creature's outburst and
instinctively unsheaths her sword.

EXT. FOREST - LATE AFTERNOON

The creature then plows into the crag shaking it from the
summit to its foundation, embracing it as if it were a tree
to be uprooted.

EXT. FOREST - CRAG - LATE AFTERNOON

One, two, three times the dragon plows into the crag pushing
its head upward and through the circling trees and foliage
with its ponderous body -- it's jaws viciously snapping air
before the two trapped mercenaries.

Then just as suddenly it's visage slips away to disappear
from their view.

Standing with her back pressed against the rising horn of the
crag, her eyes wide in horror, Valeria places a hand upon her
rising and falling bosom and tries to catch her breath.

Sitting next to her, Conan, calm, relaxes on the outcropping
rock. He then stands up and studies the erratic behavior of
the beast.

                    CONAN
              (folding arms on chest)
          The poison is doing its work.

Valeria glares at him as if he's crazy.

                    VALERIA
          That's not possible... not with a
          thing that size.

                    CONAN
          No, look at him... before he was
          just mad at being jabbed, but now
          he's really feeling it. The sounds
          he's making are not of anger. He's
          in a lot of pain... inside. Just
          look at the way he's moving.

Conan looks into her dread-and-doubt filled face and motions
with his head and eyebrows to encourage her.

                    CONAN
          Go ahead, take a look.

Valeria steps up next to him and peeks over and downward and catches a confused dragon pitching from side-to-side like a huge dreadnaught, its legs alternatively and intermittently collapsing under its ponderous bulk as it squeals and roars in agonizing pain.

                    CONAN
          If he's not blind already, he will
          be.

No sooner is he finished than his prediction takes wings.
The creature starts bumping into trees.

Conan drops his eyes on her, reflecting a slight grim grin.

                    CONAN
          You see?! It's blind already.

Abruptly the dragon turns about and makes a headlong dash through the forest trampling everything in its path, as it screams like a monstrous banshee.

                    VALERIA
               (hopeful)
          Is he leaving?

                    CONAN
          It's heading for the pool! It's
          the poison. It's making it
          thirsty. Let's go!

                    VALERIA
               (shakes head)
          I'm not going down there.

                    CONAN
          We must.
               (indicating the remains)
          Or we'll suffer his fate.

                    VALERIA
          I'm staying right here, until that
          thing's dead.

                    CONAN
          This may be are only chance to
          escape while it's filling it's
          belly. It's blind but it can still
          smell and it will return -- and
          perhaps others.

Valeria is instantly pricked into wakefulness by Conan's last word. Her worries and fears are magnified.

                         VALERIA
               Others?

                         CONAN
               Where there's one, there may be
               more. Come, woman!

Swiftly Conan descends pausing only to help Valeria, who
marvels at the Cimmerian's agility.

EXT. FOREST - NEAR SUNSET

As they touch the forest floor, the sounds of stentorious
slurping and lapping reach their ears.

                         CONAN
               The poison may or may not kill him,
               but we better not be here when he's
               finished.

Above the

CANOPY

of the endless forest, a reddish-orange sun prepares to merge
with the horizon.

BACK TO SCENE

A vague, nebulous twilight fills the inner forest as Conan
grabs Valeria by the wrist and leads her away from the crag --
his tread more silent than a whisper.

                         CONAN
                    (in low tones)
               I don't think he'll be able to
               follow us -- not unless the wind
               blows our scent to him.

                         VALERIA
                    (to self; in a subdued
                     voice)
               Mitra forbid that the wind should
               betray us now!

In the descending shadows Valeria's face appears like an
indistinct, oval pearl. Her hand clenches and unclenches the
pommel of her naked sword.

Conan's smouldering eyes glow in the gloom.

Then suddenly a tremendous snapping and rending of trees and branches fill the forest behind them.

Valeria bites her lower lip, stopping an involuntary scream.

> VALERIA
> (in a panicky whisper)
> It's after us!

Conan shakes his head moving quickly and instinctively like a disembodied spirit through the forest.

> CONAN
> (in a subdued voice)
> Our scent was gone when he
> returned...

Conan carefully pushes a branch out of their way, lets Valeria pass first still holding onto her wrist, follows, lets go of the branch gently and then retakes the lead.

> CONAN
> ... And now he's crashing into
> everything trying to find our
> spoor, but without the wind he'll
> never find us. No tree will save
> us from him. We've got to keep
> moving! The city is our only chance
> now!

EXT. FOREST - SUNSET

As they slink along towards the city, the forest before them begins to thin out and become more sparse, the rummaging din of the creature hanging behind them in the darker entanglements of the shadowy forest.

Valeria lets a sigh of relief escape and slides her sword into the scabbard as they spot the open plain not too far ahead of them.

> VALERIA
> A little further and we'll --

Conan's mane and Valeria's locks are suddenly disturbed by a wind emanating from the south.

> CONAN
> Crom!

> VALERIA
> Mitra!

The wind continues along its path, inexorably, behind them and instantly the forest reverberates with the dragon's thunderous roar, its erratic movements become a sustained crashing charge in their direction.

Conan's eyes blaze!

                    CONAN
          We've no choice! Run for it!

Conan takes off at a fast clip but maintains a pace so that Valeria can stay close to his side.

Not a landlubber, Valeria begins to tire out after the first hundred yards. The

BEAST

a huge tub of terror, breaks through thick thickets and into the more open forest, heading straight for them.

CONAN

noting Valeria's predicament and without breaking his stride, wraps a mighty arm around her winsome waist, lifts the amazed girl off the ground and opens up, his powerful long

LEGS

eating up the ground beneath them.

CONAN

shoots a quick glance behind him only to see that the

DRAGON

is gaining ground on them.

CONAN

hurls Valeria from him through the air some fifteen feet landing her at the base of one of the trees.

VALERIA

sits up light-headed to see Conan turn about and face the
steamrolling onslaught of destruction.

Fearlessly, Conan dashes towards the dragon, broadsword
unsheathed.

IN SLOW MOTION

Before they collide Conan leaps into the air, both hands
gripping the sword high above his head and strikes downward
to cut deep past the scales of its snout.

Conan is then struck by the behemoth's massive shoulder that
sends him flying through the air, sword still in-hand, to
land rolling and tumbling fifty feet away.

BACK TO NORMAL SPEED

Conan rolls up onto his feet and hurries to Valeria, a little
off-balance. He finds her sitting and dazed but otherwise
unscathed by the monster.

Together they follow the creature barreling through the
sparse forest like a runaway locomotive only to be stopped by
a colossal tree, the impact of which crushes its skull like
an eggshell and uproots the tree.

For a few moments it stands on its massive short legs, its
pulped head unrecognizable, and then drops straight down
dead.

Following suit, the forest giant falls over the vanquished
reptile covering it completely, the death throes of the
creature shaking its shroud of branches, intermittently.

Then stillness.

Conan shakes his black mane to clear his head, sheathes his
broadsword and with an outstretched hand helps Valeria back
to her feet.

Together they endeavor to jog towards the open plain,
stumbling like drunken sailors, as they try to regain their
equilibrium.

EXT. PLAIN - TWILIGHT

As they cross into the treeless plain, Conan turns and faces the black forest and shakes his head slowly, mystified at the strangeness.

The only sound that reaches his ears is silence. No bird cries. No barks, coughs or roars. No life whatsoever. Not even the rustling of branches or leaves. Nothing.

Conan turns about and takes the girl's hand and Valeria does not complain or resist.

> CONAN
> Let's go... and pray our scent is
> not picked up by others. Or
> else....

Conan shrugs as she glances up at him -- the last vestiges of light in her eyes reflecting her apprehension at the implication.

EXT. PLAIN - DUSK

A mile from the forest and still some distance from the city with no sound or sight of pursuit, Valeria's self-confidence returns. Her fears and nervousness all but gone.

The darkening sky, aided by the stars and a rising moon, manages to illuminate the landscape, somewhat, exposing the silhouette forms of the cacti dotting the plain.

> CONAN
> (shakes head; stumped)
> I don't understand it. How can
> anyone live there without cattle or
> crops of any kind. It doesn't make
> any sense.

> VALERIA
> Maybe it's all kept in the rear of
> the city.

> CONAN
> (mutters)
> Maybe, but I doubt it. There was
> no sign of either from the crag.

Silently, they push on towards the barely discernable city.

EXT. PLAIN - NIGHT

The yellow moon rising to the left of the city gives shape to menacing, black towers and ramparts and Valeria shivers reflexively at the sight of them.

Conan senses her negative reaction and he too glances at the black monoliths and high walls, winces and stops.

> CONAN
> We'll sleep out here tonight.

EXT. PLAIN - CACTUS ATOLL - NIGHT

He leads Valeria to a group of cactuses that grow in a circular fashion like an atoll. Its walls are made of compacted tubular, spiny cactuses pressed close together like a palisaded wall at just under four feet in height.

> CONAN
> There's no sense in trying to gain
> entrance at night... it's dangerous
> enough during the day.

Conan pulls out his sword and begins hacking an entrance into the cactus atoll.

> CONAN
> At best, they probably wouldn't let
> us in... and at worst they'd fill
> us with arrows.

Conan finishes cutting an opening and returns his great sword to its scabbard.

> CONAN
> Anyway, we need to sleep and since
> we don't know what to expect
> tomorrow at the gate, we need to be
> at our best for whatever they may
> throw at us.

Conan motions for her to enter.

Uneasy, she glances at the opening and then towards the forest some six miles away. A spectre of fear crosses her oval face.

> CONAN
> Snakes won't trouble us in here.

                         VALERIA
                    (gulps)
               What about dragons?

                         CONAN
               Don't worry about them...
                    (turns face towards city)
               ... we'll keep watch.

Valeria nods and enters the armored cactus chamber.

Conan's eyes squint at the inky black towers and walls
outlined by the rising moon. No lights or hints of sounds
from within the city give any indication of life.

                         CONAN
               You can sleep now. I'll take the
               first watch.

Valeria, suspicious as a wildcat, hesitates but only for a
moment.

She watches as Conan sits, his back to her, outside the
entrance cross-legged with his naked broadsword across his
knees, facing the city.

Surrounded by the spiked walls of the cacti, Valeria lies
down in the giving sand.

After several moments she raises her head.

                         VALERIA
               Wake me when the moon hangs high.

Conan doesn't respond and Valeria relaxes her head back onto
her hands.

Her lovely eyes take in Conan's powerful form, statuesque in
its rigidity, picked out by the moony and starry sky, as he
guards the opening -- and then they close.

                                   MATCH CUT TO:

EXT. PLAIN - CACTUS ATOLL - DAWN

A pair of eyes are thrown open. For a moment only, are her
eyes seemingly lost, then she remembers as she spies Conan
squatting busily cutting up thick cactus leaves and pulling
out the spines.

                         VALERIA
                    (sits up to one side)
               Why didn't you wake me?!

                    CONAN
          You needed the sleep...

Conan begins paring the thick, succulent cactus leaves.

                    CONAN
          ... And being a pirate, your
          backside must have been terribly
          sore from too long in the saddle.

                    VALERIA
          And you didn't?

Conan pauses.

                    CONAN
          Before I was a pirate, I was a
          Kozak...
               (begins paring again)
          ... Kozaks live in the saddle. Our
          eyes sleep, but not our ears.

Valeria scrutinizes the calm, giant Cimmerian, and Conan
appears as reinvigorated as if he'd slept beside her all
night exhibiting no signs of haggardness or fatigue.

Conan finishes paring and hands Valeria a juicy cactus leaf.

                    CONAN
          Sink your teeth into that. It's
          food and drink. When I was chief
          of the Zuagirs, I ate a lot of
          these.

Valeria cocks her head and frowns looking at him
questioningly and Conan answers her silent query.

                    CONAN
          Zuagirs are desert men. They live
          by robbing caravans.

Valeria nods, satisfied with his answer, and bites into the
juicy cactus leaf, the juices flowing from the corners of her
mouth.

She wipes the juices away with her sleeve and looks at him
and plies Conan with a playful, mocking voice -- admiration
hidden in her eyes.

                    VALERIA
          What haven't you been?

                         CONAN
                    (mouth full)
               King... I've never been a Hyborian
               king.

Conan grins and bites off a huge chunk from the cactus leaf
and swallows it quickly, wolf-like.

                         CONAN
               But I'll be that someday -- who's
               to stop me?

Valeria shakes her head and smiles at his daring and
confident boldness and then takes another bite of her
delicious cactus leaf.

Conan washes his hands in the sand and stands up.

                         CONAN
                    (strapping on sword)
               Well, it's time we made our way to
               the city gate. If we have to fight
               them, I'd rather do it before the
               sun gets too high.

Valeria, following his example, rises and girds her rounded
hips with her sword belt.

                         CONAN
                    (smiling)
               Here's your dagger.

Conan extends the dagger hilt first. Valeria raises an
eyebrow, then looks down at her empty sheath, takes the blade
and returns it into place.

EXT. PLAIN - DAWN

Side by side they march off together leaving behind the spiny
makeshift fortress.

Conan glances down at his companion, enjoying Valeria's
swaggering stride that matches his own.

                         CONAN
               You move more like a hillman than a
               pirate. You're Aquilonian, aren't
               you?

Pleased by his interest and praising tone, she nods.

                    VALERIA
          Yes, I was born and bred
          Aquilonian... born and bred.

                    CONAN
          Your white skin never darkened
          under the sun of Darfar -- and
          never will. You'd be the envy of
          many a princess I've met.

Valeria restrains a smile as her eyes glimpse his smouldering
blue-eyes, taking a clandestine delight in the Cimmerian's
compliment.

EXT. PLAIN - MORNING

As they near the city the sun rises, its showering rays
turning the towers and ramparts into glowing, bloody-red
hues.

Conan squints and scowls as he surveys the lofty towers,
ramparts, and battlements.

                    CONAN
          Last night they were as black as
          Stygia... today they're as red as
          blood. I don't like it.

Conan studies the ground around him and before him as they
approach the city.

                    CONAN
          No signs of cattle... not even a
          road on this side... and the ground
          hasn't been plowed in ages -- but
          look, it must have been cultivated
          at one time.

Conan points and Valeria follows his long arm to ancient
ditches partially filled in some places or covered by
cactuses.

Valeria's eyes stretch out across the expansive plain on all
sides of the city, only to be stopped by the encircling
forest fringes ensnaring it.

Her troubled gaze shifts towards the battlements. No
gleaming helmets or spears reflect the early morning light.
Just like the forest, utter silence reigns uncontested.

EXT. XUCHOTL - NORTHERN WALL - GATE - MORNING (LATER)

The sun hangs higher in the eastern sky granting the towering ramparts the power to cast shadows upon the grounds.

Within these shadows, Conan and Valeria finally end their trek across the plain to confront a colossal bronze gate.

No alarms or challenges greet them.

Mottled rust covers the iron bracings and thick sticky layers of spiderwebs smother the hinges, the bolted panel and the sill.

> VALERIA
> (astonished)
> This gate's been closed for ages!

Conan nods.

> CONAN
> An empty city -- dead. No wonder
> there were no cattle or crops.

> VALERIA
> But why? Why would they leave such
> a great city -- and who built it?

Conan moves back a few paces and looks up at the battlements shielding his eye with both hands and then rejoins Valeria, shaking his head, puzzled at the oddity.

> CONAN
> There's no telling. Maybe war...
> maybe a plague -- who knows. As to
> the builders... perhaps Stygians,
> but I doubt it. The architecture
> is different.

Valeria's eyes narrow at a sudden thought.

> VALERIA
> Mitra! There may still be treasure
> inside for the taking! I don't
> know about you, but I'd like to go
> in and find out.

They look at each other. Valeria eager and hopeful. Conan, his brows knit, pondering the wisdom of her desire.

> VALERIA
> What have we got to lose?

Conan regards the enormous gate, glances at Valeria, shrugs, and then presses a mighty shoulder against it. He strains with all the power of his legs and shoulder and after several moments of prodigious effort, it gives, unexpectedly.

Slowly, the enormous gate begins to swing inward, its hinges grating and creaking against every inch.

INT. XUCHOTL - GREAT HALL - MORNING

Once open, Conan draws his sword and enters followed closely from behind by Valeria, who, looking over his shoulder, inhales a gasp of utter surprise at the unexpected sight.

The gate is no more than a door that opens into a hallway of epic dimensions -- both in width and in length. Its length is so, that its end, vague at best, seems indiscernible from their location.

The floor is covered with square, stone tiles that seem to emanate a smoldering, fiery glow from beneath them, as if they were a window to a river of flowing volcanic magma.

The walls are green and glossy.

Conan touches the wall with his free hand.

                    CONAN
          By Crom! I'm a Shemite, if these
          walls aren't solid jade!

                    VALERIA
               (incredulous)
          That can't be! There's too much of
          it for it to be jade.

                    CONAN
          I've plundered too many Khitan
          caravans not to know the difference
          -- and that's jade!

Conan looks up and Valeria follows his eyes.

The vaulted ceiling made of the brilliant, deep blue of lapis lazuli hangs above them and embedded in that blue, and throughout, are countless clustered stones, that radiate a greenish, noxious effulgence -- as if alive and watching.

                    VALERIA
          I've never seen anything like it.

              CONAN
                (scowling)
        The natives of Punt call them green
        fire-stones. They believe them to
        be the petrified eyes of ancient
        pre-historic snakes known as the
        Golden Serpents...

He places the point of his sword on the floor and rests both
hands on the pommel, standing there like a great crusader.

              CONAN
        ... And at night they glow much
        stronger, like the eyes of a cat
        and this hallway will be lit up in
        a queer, ghoulish light.

Conan resheaths his broadsword.

              CONAN
        Now, let's see about that treasure.

              VALERIA
                (worried)
        Close the door first.

Conan meets her eyes with knit brows.

              VALERIA
        The last thing I want is to be
        chased down this hallway by another
        dragon... once was enough.

Conan tries to suppress a barbaric grin.

              CONAN
        I doubt if they ever leave the
        forest.

Conan shoulders the monstrous door and pushes. It swings
slowly but much easier and with less noise than the first
time.

After closing the portal Conan discovers a broken bolt.

              CONAN
        This must be what I felt snap when
        I was forcing it open. It's almost
        rusted through... but you can tell
        it just broke.

Valeria moves in to get a better view.

                    CONAN
          Why would an abandoned city be
          bolted from within?

                    VALERIA
          More than likely they used a
          different door.

                    CONAN
               (nodding)
          Maybe.

Light filters into the hall from large rectangular skylights,
made from crystal-like material, spaced intermittently high
up along the spine of the ceiling.

As they enter the darkened areas between the skylights, the
green-jeweled orbs blink like the stars in the night sky
watching them as they traverse the smoldering lake of fire
beneath their feet, the stone tiles ever changing in their
dull, fiery radiance.

On both sides of the Great Hall, balustraded galleries rise
three levels, one upon the other.

Conan scrutinizes the stacked galleries.

                    CONAN
               (mutters to self)
          Hmm, four stories.
               (to Valeria)
          They probably lead straight up to
          the roof.

Conan then turns his attention to the far end of the hallway.

                    CONAN
          This hall is longer than most city
          streets I've ridden through... and
          there's another door at the other
          end.

Valeria squints and blinks her eyes open and shut a few times
attempting see the door but shakes her head unable to make it
out.

                    VALERIA
          My cutthroats deem me keen-eyed,
          but they're no match for yours, if
          you can see that door from here.

Passing several doors, they finally turn into an open one.

MONTAGE - CHAMBERS AND HALLWAYS

1) Conan and Valeria shuffle through windowless chambers with
walls varying from jade, chalcedony and marble to ivory.

2) The only light in their exploration through these chambers
and corridors emanates from the, now, intense and sinister
fire-stones above them and from the fiery flames beneath
them.

3) The chambers, some adorned with silken rugs, are clean
except for the occasional corner cobweb. No dust can be
detected on the floors nor on the seats or tables made from
marble, carnelian or jade.

4) Under this sorcerous light they continue, chamber-to-
chamber -- avoiding the pitch black ones -- or chamber-to-
hallway with the halls varying in size, length and
brightness.

5) Each and every door they open inescapably leads to another
chamber or hallway.

INT. XUCHOTL - STAIRCASE CHAMBER - HOURS LATER

They enter a chamber with an ivory staircase spiraling
upwards, the walls banded with friezes.

                    VALERIA
                (frustrated)
          Where the hell are the streets?
          I'm sick of this. This place is
          bigger than the seraglio of Turan.

Conan's mind is on something else.

                    CONAN
                (thinking aloud)
          It couldn't have been a plague.
          Where are the skeletons? Maybe it
          was sorcery or maybe --

                    VALERIA
          -- Damn the "maybes!" Who knows?
          I for one don't care.

He ignores her tantrum and moves in on a frieze for a closer
inspection, Valeria shadowing beside him.

                    VALERIA
          Who are they?

Conan cons it carefully. The frieze shows a group of
slender, fine-featured men and women dressed in thin robes,
jewelled and feasting.

Conan frowns and shakes his thick black mane.

>   CONAN
>   I've never seen their like, yet
>   they bear the stamp of the East.
>   Vendhya or Kosala, perhaps... that
>   would be my guess.

Valeria's interest is piqued but she disguises it with a
mocking tone.

>   VALERIA
>   Don't tell me you were king of
>   Kosala.

Conan is not troubled in the least by her manner and answers
plainly.

>   CONAN
>   Of the Kosalans, no -- but I was
>   chief of the Afghulis for a time...
>   up in the Himalayan mountains where
>   they border the kingdom of Vendhya.

Conan glances at another frieze depicting the same clean-cut
people -- this time dancing.

>   CONAN
>   (studying the frieze)
>   The more I look at them the more
>   they remind me of the Kosalans --
>   but why they would come this far
>   west and build a city is a mystery
>   to me.

Conan's gaze shifts to another frieze and he grins.

>   CONAN
>   They're definitely from the East...

The frieze depicts the same people love-making.

>   CONAN
>   (looking at Valeria)
>   ... But from what kingdom, I can't
>   say for certain. They must have
>   lived very boring lives, though...
>   there aren't any scenes of battles
>   or wars.

                    VALERIA
          When you live this far from
          civilization, there are no
          enemies... except maybe dragons.

                    CONAN
          There are always enemies.

Conan gives the staircase a quick glance.

                    CONAN
          Let's see where this leads.

INT. XUCHOTL - IVORY STAIRCASE

Together they mount the spiral staircase and ascend past
three floors and debouch into a large chamber upon the fourth
floor.

INT. XUCHOTL - FOURTH FLOOR - STAIRCASE CHAMBER - DAY

The skylights above illumine the chamber keeping the
fiendish, green fire-stones at bay and the burning floor
subdued.

Conan and Valeria poke their heads into a few of the many
doors lining one side of the chamber where similarly lighted
rooms meet their eyes.

They then open a lone door, opposite the wall with many
doors, to discover a balustraded gallery hanging above a very
much smaller hallway than the first one they encountered.

                    VALERIA
               (rankled)
          Hell!

She drops down onto a carnelian bench near a wall.

                    VALERIA
          Whoever lived here, took whatever
          treasures there were, with them. I
          for one, am tired of moving through
          this endless maze of chambers.

                    CONAN
          We don't know that and we won't
          find it staying here. At least, on
          this floor, the light is better.
          Now, to find a window with a view
          of the city. Come on, let's try
          this one.

                    VALERIA
          Search without me. I'm staying
          put...
               (winces)
          ... these aching feet of mine need
          rest.

Conan gives her an indifferent glance and disappears behind
the selected door.

Valeria leans her shoulders back against the wall and muses,
with her hands cupping the back of her head, and her boots
stretched out before her, one over the other.

The dull, burning floor, the mild twinkling of the green cat-
eyes above and the rising and falling of her bosom, are the
only perceptible movements in the room.

A sudden fragile sound wafts into the room and Valeria
instinctively shoots up onto her feet, knees bent with sword
drawn -- fully on guard.

Her ocean-blue eyes are drawn towards the open door leading
to the gallery.

She slips stealthily towards the open door and into the
gallery.

INT. XUCHOTL - FOURTH FLOOR - GALLERY - DAY

Valeria crouches low and peers down between the balusters.
Her avid eyes lock-on to a man sneaking along the hallway on
the third floor.

He's naked except for a meager, silk loincloth that barely
conceals his ripped hips and is girded around the waist with
a leather belt three inches wide.

The man has a very dark complexion like that of an Indian.
His cadaverous body is equipped with small, bunched muscles
without the smoothness of any symmetry -- almost repellent.

His long black hair hangs lifeless scraping his shoulders as
he treads the flaming floor half crouched. His manner wary --
his head turning this way and that.

Valeria's astonishment gives way to one of puzzlement as she
catches his arm trembling, wielding a wide-tipped, curved
sword in a desperate grip.

An inexplicable terror enshrouds the man as he turns his head
in her direction, his eyes blazing wildly with fear.

The tormented man, on stealthy feet, disappears into an open chamber below and beside Valeria's gallery.

Seconds later the hall is filled with a partial cry that is quickly snuffed out.

Valeria, startled, freezes in place.

Utter stillness reigning anew, Valeria creeps along the gallery until she comes to a door above the chamber entered by the man.

She pauses a moment, then opens the door carefully. She pauses again to look within, then enters.

INT. XUCHOTL - FOURTH FLOOR - CIRCULAR GALLERY - DAY

Valeria finds herself in another, but smaller, gallery that encircles a larger chamber below it, illuminated only by the eerie green radiance of the fire-stones embedded in a ceiling lower than that of the hall.

Valeria eases over to the balustrade and peers over it.

In the gloomy chamber below, she sees the body of a man lying face down on a red carpet with his arms outstretched and his curved blade near his sword arm.

Her eyebrows rise as she recognizes the same man as the one who, a moment ago, entered the chamber.

As she scans the floor below her, she narrows her eyes and discovers a wet, deeper, darker red that appears to be expanding in size from beneath the prone man.

Valeria drops down and hugs the balustrade, a quick quiver running through her shoulders.

Her eyes search the dark shadows beneath the jutting balcony that are unreachable by the twinkling green eyes above her, but nothing materializes.

Then her quick eyes are arrested by the sudden entrance of another man, similar to the one on the floor, from a door opposite the one that leads out into the hall.

The STUPEFIED MAN's eyes stare down at the unmoving body and against his very will, he opens his trembling mouth and stammers like a machine gun.

                    STUPEFIED MAN
          Ch-Ch-Ch-Ch-Chicmec!

He waits for a response but there is none.

He pads over to the body and kneeling beside it grasps a shoulder with a shaky hand and pulls it up at an angle to one side.

Chicmec's dead head drops back exposing a deep slit on the throat running from ear-to-ear.

                    STUPEFIED MAN
          Ah!

The Stupefied Man, as if stung by a scorpion, instantly releases his grip on the shoulder and the corpse falls face down to wallow in its blood again.

He snaps up shaking like a tattered rag in the wind, his face blanched -- his eyes filled with horror.

He gulps and, as he prepares to flee, suddenly becomes stock-still.

Valeria follows the petrified man's hopeless stare across to the other side, where under the shadow of the balcony another light, unlike the green cat-eyes gleaming above, begins to materialize.

At first the slow, pulsing light is faint but steadily it strengthens and begins to expand.

Valeria looks away, blinks her eyes and returns her dismayed eyes back towards the light and there in its midst, is a deformed human skull from which the light seems to originate.

Blanketed in the shadows the skull seems to float in mid-air intensifying all the while.

Slowly, it moves from beneath the gallery followed by a distorted, unsightly shadow that morphs into the figure of a man with his arms and torso bleached white to match the grinning, fiendish skull surrounded by an ethereal halo.

The man stands frozen in place his eyes glazed over as in a hypnotic trance. His sword hangs lifeless from his limp arm. His expression, bewitched.

The eyeless, grinning skull stops before the hapless man, its pulsating light affecting even Valeria, who shakes her head to ward off its affects, her beautiful locks disturbed.

The Stupefied Man's sword slips from his grasp to the floor and, like a possessed man, drops down to his knees, his head and arms hanging limply as he awaits the end.

The gleam of a sword appears in the hand of the ghostly spectre.

Valeria's ire rises as it raises the sword above the bowed, paralyzed man's neck and in one quick motion she leaps over the balustrade.

INT. XUCHOTL - THIRD FLOOR - CHAMBER OF TEZCOTI - CONTINUOUS

She lands with drawn sword almost soundlessly, but the pulsating skull hears it nonetheless and spins about to face the interloper.

Valeria strikes like a flash of lightning cutting through his shoulder, breast bone and spine, her eyes lighting up as she discovers mere flesh and bone beneath her blade.

The screaming ghostly figure collapses in a heap and the pulsating, grinning skull rolls away revealing a man similar to the one she saved, his face contorted in spasmodic death throes with flooding blood spilling from his mouth.

The kneeling man, awakening but still in a state of stupor, shakes his head.

He stares at the corpse of his late nemesis and then at Valeria's bleeding sword and finally looks up at the girl standing over the body, gaping in catatonic disbelief.

Picking up his sword, he struggles to his feet with a torrent of questions.

                    STUPEFIED MAN
          Who are you -- where did you come
          from -- why are you here, in
          Xuchotl?

So overwhelmed by his nervous and exultant state of mind, he doesn't wait for a reply.

                    STUPEFIED MAN
               (raving to self)
          No matter!
               (looking at Valeria)
          Surely a friend, you must be!
               (looking at the corpse)
          Why else would you kill the Burning
          Skull?!

                    VALERIA
               (perplexed)
          Stygian? How is it you speak their
          tongue?

Oblivious to her question he presses on.

                    STUPEFIED MAN
          For so long we believed it a
          creature conjured up from the
          depths of the catacombs, and it's
          only a man!

                    VALERIA
          Who and --

He holds up a hand for silence.

                    STUPEFIED MAN
          They come!

He freezes in place and cocks his head listening intently.

Valeria shifts her weight to one leg, throws a hand on a
generous hip and thinking him mad, intimates, with a slight
motion of her head, that she hears nothing.

                    STUPEFIED MAN
               (in intense low tones)
          We dare not remain here.

He listens a moment longer.

                    STUPEFIED MAN
               (in intense low tones)
          From east of the Great Hall they
          come...

He glances around like a cornered, wounded animal.

                    STUPEFIED MAN
          ... And may be upon us, even now!

He grabs her wrist in a fearful grip, from which Valeria
frees herself with no little effort.

                    VALERIA
          Who are these people?

He stares at her confounded, as if not understanding the
question.

                    STUPEFIED MAN
          Our enemies... the Xotalancas.
          They dwell on the eastern side of
          the Great Hall.

He points to the enemy's body lying in a great pool of blood.

                    STUPEFIED MAN
          He is one of them... and more are
          coming.

                    VALERIA
               (taken aback)
          But I thought this city was
          deserted -- people live here?

The man trembles like a newborn foal.

                    STUPEFIED MAN
          Yes, now come! Follow me to
          Tecuhltli!

He takes hold of her wrist once more and pulls her towards
his original entry point, his darting eyes fear-filled, his
face and forehead covered in thick sweat.

She throws off his offending grip.

                    VALERIA
               (vexed)
          If you touch me again, for whatever
          reason, I'll lop off your head!

Taking stock of her temperament, he takes hold of himself,
somewhat.

                    VALERIA
          I want to know who you are and
          where you were trying to take me
          against my will -- and what in,
          Mitra's name, is going on?!

He shifts his intense eyes in all directions and then his
words shoot out at breakneck speed, almost incoherently.

                    STUPEFIED MAN
          I am Techotl of Tecuhltli...

TECHOTL points his sword at the man with the split throat.

                    TECHOTL/STUPEFIED MAN
          ... As was my comrade. We came to
          the Halls of Silence seeking to
          ambush the Xotalancas but became
          separated in this treacherous maze
          and here I found him with his
          throat cut.

He drops his chin down to his chest and shakes his head in a
moment of mourning, then just as suddenly his head is up
again, his eyes blazing.

                    TECHOTL
          The Burning Skull, it was, that
          killed him. Just as sure as he
          would have killed me, if not for
          your timely aid. But he is not
          alone. Others are, even now,
          creeping upon us as we speak. If
          they come, be prepared to fight to
          the death! Better to die fighting
          them than to be taken alive -- even
          our gods tremble at such a fate!

At the mere mention of it, his body shivers and his
complexion pales a touch, under the radiant green- eyes.

Puzzled, Valeria studies him for a moment and then turns her
attention towards the Burning Skull.

The Burning Skull throbs and pulses on its side grinning at
the girl as she extends the tip of her boot towards it.

Techotl lurches forward abruptly, horrified.

                    TECHOTL
          Touch it not! And let not your
          eyes fall upon it! Its gaze will
          take your mind -- and your soul!
          To touch it brings insanity and
          death! Only the Xotalanc sorcerers
          know its secrets and how to wield
          its power. It was they who brought
          it forth from its eons of burial in
          the catacombs... where the ancient
          bones of Xuchotl's dark kings lie.

Valeria glares at him and her narrowing eyes meet his
terrified ones, behind which seems to reside an indefinable
trace of lingering lunacy.

Desperately, Techotl, importunes her.

                    TECHOTL
          We must flee before all is lost.
          Come!

He reaches for her hand, but suddenly remembering her threat
of decapitation, he jerks his hand back as if bitten by some
unseen creature and for the first time regards her.

                    TECHOTL
          I do not know from where you came
          to be here, but you are neither
          demon nor god, or you would know
          this.
                    (MORE)

                    TECHOTL (CONT'D)
          Perhaps from the east, like our
          ancestors -- but no matter. You
          killed my enemy and now you are my
          friend and a friend to all
          Tecuhltli. Follow me quickly
          before we perish at the hands of
          the Xotalancas!

Valeria turns away from his offensive features to stare at
the Burning Skull.

VALERIA'S TRANCE - INT. XUCHOTL - CHAMBER OF TEZCOTI

A surreal fog spreads and surrounds the pulsing, distorted,
human yet inhuman, Burning Skull. The flaming floor and the
fire-stones are no longer.

Its empty eye sockets suddenly flash to life like two
blinding suns.

The Burning Skull rises above the mist and hovers, boring
into her eyes.

Spellbound by the grinning skull, the light of her eyes
begins to fade -- to die.

The jaws of the fantastic entity begin to snap open and shut.
Slowly at first, then they speed up, the snapping heightening
to a tumultuous din.

The snapping stops and the malignant distended jaws erupt
into a volcanic, scandalous, echoing laughter that sways and
shakes the entire chamber.

Valeria's eyes are shock-open. Nausea and dizziness begin to
overwhelm her as she struggles to keep her footing, yet she's
unable to break free from the grip of the Burning Skull's
hellish, throbbing eyes.

To her, the ghostly skull appears almost transparent. She
covers her ears to stop the pain from the rising abysmal
laughter, the room continues to waver in a mind bending
convulsion.

Yet her eyes are held fast by the hovering skull -- the light
within them, fading.

A faint voice enters the vacuum of suspended time. The voice
crawls through the illusory world trying desperately to make
itself heard. The surreal voice strengthens and cries out to
her.

                         TECHOTL (V.O.)
                Look away! Do not look at its
                eyes!

The voice breaks the spell and the Burning Skull roars, in
rage, shaking the chamber from floor to ceiling.

BACK TO SCENE

Valeria, still tranced, closes her eyes as she places a hand
on her forehead. She shakes her golden locks vigorously like
a lion's mane.

When she opens them, her eyes are clear and free again, with
Techotl still rambling on.

                         TECHOTL
                ... The skull, long ago, belonged
                to a king sorcerer... And though
                dead, it still lives drawing its
                fiery power from the outer worlds!

More than convinced, Valeria snarls, steps quickly towards
the skull with her naked, bloody sword and with a single
blow, shatters the Burning Skull into countless fiery
smithereens.

From an unseen void a hideous, raging cry rips through the
chamber and then dissipates with a dying moan.

Techotl, aghast, stares at the scattered glowing pieces until
their fiery light goes out.

Forgetting himself, he grabs hold of Valeria's upper arm and
looks into her beautiful face.

                         TECHOTL
                  (in awe)
                You killed it! You have crushed
                forever the power of the Burning
                Skull... and no sorcery of the
                Xotalancas can restore it!

Remembering their peril and her admonition he lets go of her
arm.

                         TECHOTL
                Follow me, now! We must leave this
                place!

Valeria shakes her lovely head.

                         VALERIA
              Not yet. I'm not alone. I must
              wait until --

Valeria sees Techotl turn rigid, his eyes transfixed and
blazing with a hint of madness as they look past the girl.

Valeria, alerted, spins around just in time to meet the
silent onslaught of four men, who rush in from four separate
entrances to charge upon them in the center of the chamber.

Except for the white skull drawn on their chests, all of them
are facsimiles of Techotl, with lank, long hair and small
potato-sized muscles protruding from their ripped spare
bodies -- dressed and armed exactly alike.

Techotl rushes forward to engage the foremost, ducks beneath
a slicing blade and takes the man down where they struggle
for the upper hand in a desperate silence.

The remaining dark-eyed devils attack the tall woman almost
simultaneously, but like a hellcat she's among them swirling
her singing blade in a dizzying display of incomparable
swordplay.

To quick to follow, she flicks her straight, double-edged
sword and taps aside the wide sword of the nearest antagonist
and lays open his throat to a gushing torrent of blood.

Like a whirlwind she dances about them dodging thrusts and
parrying, her eyes alive with the joy of martial action --
her full, shapely lips smiling in anticipation of the kill.

Valeria parries a blow from the taller man, kicks him
backward and parries an attack from the shorter man,
counterattacks with a feint, the man attempts to parry and
she drills his midsection with her unforgiving sword.

As the wounded man falls to his knees in excruciating pain,
the taller man leaps forward with a series of vicious
downward blows driving her back and making it virtually
impossible for her to muster a counter.

She backs up, fully in control, as she bides her time for an
opening.

A quick glance, and she spies Techotl atop his opponent
frantically striving to drive a dagger into the enemy's
heart.

Slowly she leads the perspiring and tiring Xotolanc backwards
until her mobility is suddenly impaired.

She glances down to her left to discover the wounded man wrapped tightly around her leg.

Emboldened by her handicap, the taller cries out in exultation and drives Valeria back with terrific blows; yet, she blocks and parries them while dragging the cleaving, wounded man along with her.

The wounded man crawls up her leg, high enough, to clamp down his teeth on her exposed, lower thigh and Valeria, with a snarl, grips his long hair in an angry left hand and yanks his head backwards.

His strong white teeth and crazed blood-red eyes glare up at her as she struggles to hold off the tall assailant.

The taller man, feeling victory close at hand, redoubles his efforts and strikes down towards her head with a mighty blow.

Valeria catches the downward arc of the wide sword just barely, but the force of it drops the flat of her blade on her head like a hammer.

Lights flash before her and she stumbles.

The taller man raises his sword high for the final stroke, his mad face in the throes of triumphant ecstasy and through his lips passes a victorious cry!

Out of nowhere, a towering shadow materializes without warning behind the exultant Xotolanc and faster than light and with tremendous force, a huge, gleaming broadsword cleaves his head in half down to his neck -- his cry of victory, trapped in his throat.

Brains, blood, and gore jettison from his broken skull as he drops to the floor and into oblivion.

Valeria recovers from the daze and her sight returns.

                    VALERIA
          Conan!

In a wave of fury she turns her attention to the wounded man still in the grasp of her left hand.

In a flash, she pulls his head back and with an upward swing of her sword she severs the head from the body.

The body collapses twitching and spouting blood.

With a yell of passion she pitches the head across the chamber and turns to meet the Cimmerian.

Conan, amazed and bewildered, stands -- with his blood-stained sword hanging from his powerful arm -- over the dead body.

                    CONAN
          From what hell did these dogs come
          from?

Valeria makes a face and shrugs with gesturing hand, helpless to answer his question.

Conan's eyes move from Valeria to Techotl.

A blade is wrenched from the heart of a body still in its death throes. Blood bubbles from the terminal wound.

Techotl, drenched in sweat, rises from the vanquished Xotolanc and shakes the blood from the dagger.

As he stands he grimaces.

One of his thighs bleeds from a deep knife wound.

His grimace switches to surprise at the unexpected sight of the giant Cimmerian.

Conan's steady, stern eyes watch Techotl carefully.

Techotl's strange, almost hypnotic eyes blaze in triumphant glee.

                    TECHOTL
          Five red nails! Five more to
          celebrate the death of these vermin
          dogs! We must thank the gods for
          this victory!

He raises his hands up high in homage looking up towards the glowing green ceiling and moments later he's stamping, kicking and spitting upon their faces and bodies, his features filled with unbridled hate, as he dances about them.

Conan and Valeria watch Techotl's wicked dance in unfeigned amazement and without looking at the girl...

                    CONAN
          Who is this lunatic?

Valeria shakes her head and gestures with a hand.

                    VALERIA
          I'm not sure, but by what he's told
          me so far, there seems to be two
          different groups that live on
          opposite sides of this strange
          city...
               (looks at the dead bodies)
          ... that really, hate each other.

                    CONAN
               (grins)
          There's nothing strange about that.

Techotl, hearing the strange language being spoken, stops his
victory dance and cocking his head like a perched raptor,
listens -- his eyes weird and aglaze.

                    VALERIA
          His name is Techotl, and he's much
          friendlier than the dead ones.

Conan spreads his thins lips across his scarred face and
silently chuckles.

                    TECHOTL
               (in low tones)
          Quickly, my friends! Before these
          dead curs are missed... and then
          many will come. Perhaps too many,
          even for your swords. Tecuhltli is
          far from here... but, once there,
          they will welcome you and reward
          you for what you have done for me.
          Five red nails! Why, they won't
          believe it -- but they will when
          they see you!

                    CONAN
               (mutters)
          Let's be off then.

Techotl hastens through one of the many doors followed by
Valeria and Conan.

Conan canvasses the chamber one last time and then closes the
door behind him leaving behind a bloody morgue.

INT. XUCHOTL - FOURTH FLOOR - LONG CORRIDOR - LATE AFTERNOON

Under intermittent sheets of light from the skylights and the
gleaming glow of cat-eyes clustered about the lapis lazuli
ceiling, like green stars in a mystical midnight blue sky,
Techotl leads them cautiously along the flaming floor with
Conan and Valeria, abreast of each other, following close
behind.

                    VALERIA
               (in a low voice)
          What is this place? Better yet,
          what have we stumbled upon?

                    CONAN
          Crom, skin me, if I know! One
          thing I do know, his kind didn't
          build this city. They're from the
          shores of Lake Zuad, near the Kush
          border... they're known as
          Tlazitlans... a cross between
          Stygians and an eastern race that
          came to Stygia long ago.

As they steal along the endless corridor flanked by
innumerable chambers, Techotl pauses now and again and cocks
his head to listen for sounds of pursuit only to quickly
resume his scrambling gait, peering into every open doorway
they come to with fearful and fiery eyes.

Behind Techotl and watching his wary and fearful behavior, a
negligible quiver runs up Valeria's spine, contracting her
shoulders and shaking her golden locks as she traverses the
flaming floor -- the weird light of the weak, winking,
emerald gems above them, creates a nameless dream of shadowy
play between the sheets of light.

Below his low, broad forehead, Conan's eyes -- ever alert --
pick up her uneasiness and he promptly closes up the gap
between them.

Feeling his nearness she turns her head slightly without
glancing at him and taking a deep breath she regains her
poise, her apprehensive eyes easing up somewhat and secretly
comforted by the giant Cimmerian's close proximity.

                    TECHOTL
               (in a distressed whisper)
          They may try to cut us off from
          Tecuhltli -- or worse yet, an
          ambush!

                         VALERIA
                    (frustrated)
          There won't be, if you lead us
          outside the palace and into the
          streets. I'm tired of this hellish
          maze.

                         TECHOTL
          There is no outside. Xuchotl has
          no streets. There are no
          courtyards, gardens or plazas.
          This entire city is a huge palace
          covered completely by a roof... the
          Great Hall is the only street-like
          corridor in our city. It cuts
          through the center of Xuchotl from
          north to south and only its gates,
          at each end, allow egress to the
          outside world.

                         CONAN
          You've lived here all your life?

                         TECHOTL
                    (nods)
          Since I was born in Tecuhltli,
          thirty-five years ago. I've never
          been outside the city -- but save
          your questions until we arrive...
          silence is everything here! In
          these chambers and halls prowl the
          very spawns of hell. Olmec will
          explain all.

INT. XUCHOTL - FOURTH FLOOR - IMMENSE CHAMBER - LATER

Except for a few large tapestries on the marble walls and a
round, solid gold table at its center with matching chairs,
the chamber is bare.

Through this, a gaunt ghoul leads them, beneath countless,
intensifying fire-stones, as they pad along the smoldering
floor.

TIGHT CORRIDOR

In Indian file, many feet tiptoe along another throbbing,
fiery floor and a careless, unsheathed sword taps the wall.

BACK TO SCENE

As they cross the enormous chamber, Conan's moody, dark
visage suddenly quickens, his eyes burning like coals.

                    CONAN
          (in a commanding voice)
     Wait!

Valeria and Techotl turn to face the Cimmerian.

                    CONAN
          (to Techotl)
     You spoke of ambushes. What are
     the chances?

Techotl cocks his head -- a habitual characteristic of his
when puzzled.

                    TECHOTL
     The chances are always high. The
     Halls of Silence is an area
     disputed by both clans and is
     always patrolled by them and by us.
     Why do you ask?

                    CONAN
     I heard the tink of steel... there
     are men somewhere ahead of us.

Techotl trembles and his teeth begin to chatter, his jaw
muscles tightening as he forces his teeth into silence.

                    VALERIA
     Could they be your people?

                    TECHOTL
          (as if out of breath)
     We cannot take that risk.

A highly agitated Techotl takes a quick left and leads them
through an open door.

INT. XUCHOTL - FOURTH FLOOR - STAIRCASE CHAMBER - CONTINUOUS

                    TECHOTL
          (in a low desperate voice)
     This stair will lead us down to a
     dark corridor beneath us!

His repellent face is covered in heavy sweat and his eyes
glow in abject fear.

                         TECHOTL
                    (shivering and out of
                     breath)
               It may be a trap to lure us
               below... but we must take that
               chance... and hope that the real
               ambush is up here.

He closes his eyes tightly and gulps.

                         TECHOTL
               Follow me, quickly!

INT. XUCHOTL - SPIRAL STAIRCASE - CONTINUOUS

Soundlessly, they descend the ivory staircase.

LATER

At the bottom of the staircase they pause to listen for
sounds of pursuit and then stare into the mouth of a murky
corridor.

INT. XUCHOTL - MURKY CORRIDOR

They glide along noiselessly like spectres in a nightmare.
Above them the scarce and scattered emerald fire-stones give
little if any illumination, etching them out a shade or two
lighter than mere silhouettes -- gritty, pallid shapes void
of distinct features.

A door creaks open slowly somewhere behind them -- the noise
magnified ten-fold by the utter silence of the corridor.

Freezing in place, three heads swiftly turn back
simultaneously towards the unexpected sound and when they
push forward again at a faster gait

VALERIA

stumbles over a dead man's skull and falls.

                         TECHOTL
                    (screeches)
               Flee for your lives!

The terror stricken Techotl dashes down the corridor with all
the speed he can muster while

CONAN

pulls Valeria up by the arm, and holding onto her, sprints
after their spooked guide and hot on their heels the

NAKED FEET

of the Xotalancas fly after them and, with the smell of blood
fresh in their nostrils, quickly begin to close the gap
between them and their prey.

INT. XUCHOTL - MURKY CORRIDOR - IVORY STAIRCASE

The frantic

TECHOTL

reaches another ivory staircase and taking a several steps up
the spiral he turns around and stretches out an arm.

                    TECHOTL
          Take my hand! Quickly, up the
          stairs! Hurry!

Valeria stretches out her arm on the run and is yanked
unceremoniously up the spiraling staircase.

CONAN

free of Valeria, turns on the lower steps to face the
onslaught of the rushing enemy.

INT. XUCHOTL - MURKY CORRIDOR

But instead of engaging the Cimmerian the

RUSHING FEET

stop suddenly near the base of the staircase -- shadowy,
stock-still men from whose midst a

HUGE SLITHERING ABOMINATION

heads towards the staircase.

INT. XUCHOTL - MURKY CORRIDOR - IVORY STAIRCASE

Conan's

FIERY EYES

narrow as his keen ears hear a heavy dragging, shuffling, slithering sound. Then an enormous

UNDULATING SHADOWY FORM

rushes up the steps towards the Cimmerian and Conan's

BROADSWORD

slices through air and monster and

BLACK BLOOD

shoots and spurts from the mysterious ill-defined creature as the blade bites into an ivory step with the sharp, ringing, sound of steel. The

WOUNDED DARK FORM

flails and whips wildly about and grazes Conan's leg which reacts as if burned.

CONAN

scowls in disgust. The

THRASHING VAGUE FORM

falls back down among the waiting men and terrible screams, from an unfortunate one, fill the gloomy hallway.

CONAN

bolts up the winding stairs with sword in-hand and, once on the landing, through an open entrance.

INT. XUCHOTL - FOURTH FLOOR - BOLTED CHAMBER - LATE AFTERNOON

Techotl slams the heavy door and throws the bolt.

He then runs across the well lighted chamber and leads Conan and Valeria to the door on the opposite side of the room.

As they pass through the further doorway with Conan bringing up the rear, the bolted door is assailed from without!

The terrible noise swiftly draws Conan's attention and he watches as the door, under tremendous pressure, creaks and curves inward -- but holds fast.

INT. XUCHOTL - FOURTH FLOOR - NARROW HALL - LATE AFTERNOON

Techotl leads the way swiftly and warily, the once dreadful fear now noticeably absent from his features.

> CONAN
> What was it that attacked me on the
> stairs?

> TECHOTL
> (without glancing back)
> Xotalancas... the Halls of Silence
> are infested with their ilk!

> CONAN
> It wasn't a man. It was big and
> kept to the floor... and when it
> touched me, after I cut it in half,
> it was colder than the frost of
> Vanaheim.
> (grins)
> I think it killed one of the men
> below me as it shook to death.

Techotl gulps, his ashen face slapped with dread. He shivers uncontrollably and breaks out into a dogtrot.

> TECHOTL
> A Crawler! A monstrous creature
> summoned from below the catacombs
> and used against us. We don't know
> what it is for certain... but it
> inflicts unspeakable deaths upon
> our people. By Set, we must move
> with all haste! If it's turned
> loose upon us, it will follow us to
> the very entrance of Tecuhltli!

> CONAN
> I don't think so... not after that
> sword cut... if anything it's
> looking for a hole to die in -- if
> it's not dead already.

                        TECHOTL
                  (yelps fearfully)
            Faster! We must move faster!

INT. XUCHOTL - EAGLE'S WAY - NEAR SUNSET

From a chamber door Techotl and the two mercenaries emerge.

Valeria glances up at the intensifying fire-stones beginning
to overtake the waning daylight.

Techotl pauses and stares at his companions. His face less
frantic.

                        TECHOTL
            This is the Eagle's Way. We are
            close now. This hallway leads to
            Tecuhltli.

They hustle along the long hall, the weakening rays of light
touching down at intervals, until they come to an enormous
bronze door.

With his eyes aglow and an outstretched arm...

                        TECHOTL
            Behold, Tecuhltli!

He pounds the door with his fist and then stares backwards
down the hall with mild apprehension creasing his face.

                        TECHOTL
            Many have died at the very foot of
            this door, thinking themselves
            safe.

                        CONAN
            Are they deaf? What are they
            waiting for?

They are watching us through the Eye and they hesitate
because of you.

Techotl strikes the door again and in a louder voice...

                        TECHOTL
            Open up! It is I, Techotl... and
            friends!
                  (looking from Conan to
                   Valeria)
            They are trying to decide whether
            or not to let us in. Once they are
            sure, they will open the door.

Conan looks down the hall and then drops his chin. His eyes
squint as he slightly turns and angles his black-maned head
to listen.

                    CONAN
               (stern)
          They better decide quickly... I can
          hear something coming this way...
          it seems to be dragging itself
          along the floor... on the other
          side of this corridor wall -- and
               (to Techotl)
          it's not a man.

Techotl's face twists into fright and he panics, as with
renewed vigor he desperately screams and pommels the huge
bronze door with both fists!

                    TECHOTL
          Open the door! The crawler comes!
          Oh, let us in, let us in! Fools!
          What are you --

Suddenly, the great bronze door swings inward slowly and
silently.

Gleaming, menacing spears held by four determined, grim-faced
Tecuhltli, greet them -- all very similar to Techotl.

But the tense moment is short-lived as the spear points are
raised.

INT. XUCHOTL - TECUHLTLI - EAGLE'S TIER - GUARDROOM - SUNSET

After entering and just before the great door closes, Conan
catches a glimpse near the end of the bleak long corridor, of
a dark form dragging itself slowly and with obvious effort
from a chamber and into the hallway.

The misbegotten abomination crawls along the floor, its
undulating mass with its bloody head twitching and jerking
all the while.

The door shuts and Conan joins Valeria to look on as Techotl,
in his exuberant salutations, verily squeezes the life out of
one of his fellows, who grins and waits until Techotl
releases him from the grateful embrace.

Large bolts are shot across the massive bronze door.

Near the door, Conan studies the Eye apparatus embedded in
the wall consisting of grouped mirrors and above it a crystal
panel for looking through, but undetectable from without.

The guards' faces betray their amazement at the presence of the Cimmerian giant and the tall, golden-haired beauty.

Techotl ignores their perplexed, questioning eyes and with a new cloak of self-assurance...

> TECHOTL
> Come with me.

Conan takes another gander at the door and then back at Techotl, troubled by the evident inactivity.

> CONAN
> Shouldn't more men be brought into
> this chamber to repel the
> Xotalancas?

> TECHOTL
> There is no need. They would never
> attempt an assault against the Door
> of the Eagle. It cannot be brought
> down. Come! It is time I brought
> you before the leaders of
> Tecuhltli.

One of the spearman opens a door opposite the entrance, that leads into a hall and closes it behind them.

INT. TECUHLTLI - EAGLE'S TIER - HALL - SUNSET

The hall is lit by the skylights and the radiating cat-eyes and as they move along, the austerity of previous chambers and hallways, is gone.

The sleek marble walls are draped with rich and ornate tapestries and likewise the throbbing magma floors are strewn with beautiful rugs.

While the intricate benches, seats and divans against the walls are topped with fine and delicate pillows of various designs.

Near the end of the hall Techotl approaches an elaborate metal door.

INT. TECUHLTLI - EAGLE'S TIER - GREAT THRONE ROOM - SUNSET

Curious tapestries hang from the beautiful and glossy ivory walls lit by the waning light of the day passing through the skylights and the quickening green light.

Thirty dusky men and women lounge about on satin and silk draped couches and divans in indistinct conversation.

The men are similar in appearance to Techotl but the women are dressed in short, fine tunics and girted with jeweled girdles. Their square-cut locks, that fall to their bare shoulders, are held together with silver circlets. They're beautiful in a strange, peculiar way.

Upon a wide ivory seat raised up by a jade dais, sit a BIG MAN and REGAL WOMAN unlike the rest.

The Big Man, dressed in an open purple robe, is huge with an enormous chest and shoulders. The sheen of his robe flickers and changes with every subtle move and the wide sleeves being drawn back, expose his ripped and massive forearms.

His long blue-black beard reaches his wide girdle and about his blue-black square-cut mane rests a jeweled circlet.

The Regal Woman beside him is even more beautiful than the others with a jewelled circlet upon her brow encircling her long, fine, jet-black hair behind her.

The man is speaking to her while she listens with her head and eyes forward.

Unannounced, without fanfare or warning, the door bursts open startling those in the lounge to their feet, who voice wonder and surprise at the unexpected guests.

The Regal Woman also springs up from the ivory throne with a startled cry escaping her gazelle-like throat.

Tall and lissom, the Regal Woman's stare falls intently upon the wondrous loveliness of Valeria, her clenched fists matching the intensity of her dark eyes -- minus the hint of madness so prevalent among her kind.

From her firm apple-sized breasts down to her small waist, she's wrapped in fine purple linen and from her jewel encrusted girdle fall two wide strips of gilded, purple linen cloths tapering to a point down past her knees -- one before her and one behind her.

The Big Man remains seated seemingly unalarmed at the abrupt appearance of the newcomers, his bearded face sedate and emotionless as he regards them.

Techotl stops before the throne with Conan and Valeria a few paces behind him.

He bows forward with his arms outstretched and palms upwards.

TECHOTL
Behold, Prince Olmec, I bring
friends from the outer world, past
the great forest.

He raises his lank-haired head to look at OLMEC and then
takes in the stares of the others within.

With all eyes upon him, he once again faces the throne with
his eyes aglaze and with a sudden burst of gloating and
overpowering ecstasy he speaks.

TECHOTL
The Burning Skull is dead!

Cries of astonishment fill the room as his clansmen exchange
brief and unsure glances while repeating the dreaded name.

Only the pair upon the throne seem unaffected.

He raises his hands to calm them down from the horror of the
spoken nemesis.

TECHOTL
Inside the Chamber of Tezcoti I
found Chicmec... his throat had
been cut open -- but before I could
leave... from the shadows came the
Burning Skull.

He gulps remembering the horrific ordeal and, managing to
draw strength from within, continues.

TECHOTL
My blood froze and --

He closes his eyes and takes a deep breath while perspiration
beads his forehead and the faces of all are aghast as they
watch him in a fearful hypnotic trance.

TECHOTL
And my will was no longer my own.
It forced me to my knees and I knew
my end had come -- when
(points at Valeria; keeps
eyes on audience)
this golden-haired woman leaped
down upon us and slew the Burning
Skull! But when the skull rolled
off it's painted body, it was only
a vile Xotalanc who had been using
the long dead powers of an ancient
wizard brought up from the pits of
the catacombs!
(MORE)

                    TECHOTL (CONT'D)
          But that power was shattered, by
          her sword, into countless shards
          within that very chamber.

                    TECHOTL
               (with palm down sweeps an
                arm outward)
          The Burning Skull is no more! It
          has been destroyed forever!

An electrical charge runs through everyone as, with one
voice, a vehement exaltation of triumph fills the Great
Throne Room.

                    TECHOTL
          But hold! There are yet more good
          tidings to speak of! While I spoke
          with the woman, four more
          Xotalancas attacked us. The woman
          slew two and I one. It was a
          bitter battle and the tide was
          against us, until this man
               (points to Conan)
          came out of nowhere and clove the
          head of the last Xotalanc for a
          total victory!

A fierce, savage jubilation stamps the faces of his
enraptured audience.

Techotl, his face aglow with fanaticism, stares behind the
throne and points towards a glistening column made of
blackest ebony and dotted with hundreds of heavy, red-headed
copper nails.

                    TECHOTL
          Five more red nails for the Pillar
          of Vengeance! Five red nails, for
          five dead Xotalancas!

OLMEC finally stirs. His dark calm eyes lock with Techotl
and with a voice like a low, rumbling thunder...

                    OLMEC/BIG MAN
          Who, are they?

Conan does not wait for the introductions and with a powerful
voice of his own...

                    CONAN
          I am Conan of Cimmeria... and this
          is Valeria, an Aquilonian pirate of
          the Red Brotherhood.
               (MORE)

                         CONAN (CONT'D)
          We're far from the army we deserted
          at the border of Darfar, and seek
          only to reach the waters of the
          west coast.

The Regal Woman standing beside Olmec erupts in a torrent of
words, her eyes blazing.

                         REGAL WOMAN
          Your eyes shall never see the coast
          again! You will remain in Xuchotl --
          forever!

Conan's feet move instinctively to a more strategic position
enabling him to watch not only the dais but everyone else in
the Great Throne Room.

Cued by Conan, Valeria becomes watchful but not alarmed; but
Conan takes no chances.

His hand crosses his mid-section and takes a strong grip on
the hilt of his broadsword, his knees slightly bent -- his
smouldering blue-eyes, surrounded by his brown and scarred
face, ready for action.

                         CONAN
                    (growls)
          What is this?! Are we prisoners?!

Olmec pulls his staring eyes from Valeria.

                         OLMEC
          Prisoners you are not... but there
          are certain obstacles that will
          make it difficult for you and your
          companion to leave the city...
          that, is what princess Tascela
          meant to say.

Olmec glances at her, but her eyes are for Valeria only.

                         OLMEC
          Meanwhile, you are both welcome in
          Tecuhltli, as our guests. All will
          be explained to you, but first you
          must eat and drink... you must be
          hungry after your ordeal with the
          Xotalancas.

Conan watches Olmec's eyes which, along with his massive arm,
motion towards a large ivory table.

Conan sweeps the room once more for any sign of treachery
with his sword hand at the ready, grunts and with Valeria
swaggering at his side, heads towards the table.

                    OLMEC
          Prepare the table!

LATER

Presiding at the table like a maitre d', a beaming Techotl,
with his thigh bound, inspects all the golden and silver
vessels and dishes brought to the table tasting all food and
drink before being placed before their guests.

While Conan eats the exotic fruit and drinks of the red wine,
his eyes frequently shift towards TASCELA, but the woman's
eyes are always towards Valeria.

From their throne they watch the two warriors of fortune as
they eat.

Olmec, 40, brooding silently under wide, dark brows.

Tascela, 25, leaning back in a dignified manner with one arm
resting on her delectable thigh and the other on the wide
ivory armrest -- the strange light of her black, limpid eyes
burning quizzically towards the lithe form of Valeria.

Behind her, an attractive, but emotionless woman, YASALA, 27,
fans Tascela ever-so-slowly with an ostrich plume.

Olmec's dark eyes come suddenly back to life.

                    OLMEC
          You have journeyed far. We have
          records of you lands... Aquilonia
          lies far to the north, past Stygia,
          Shem, Zingara and even Ophir... and
          Cimmeria, is even further north.
          You have indeed journeyed far to
          reach our city.

                    CONAN
               (munching fruit)
          Idleness is for fools... and we're
          not the sort to remain over long...
          in one place.

                    OLMEC
          Yet, it is still a mystery to me
          how you managed to come through the
          forest unscathed.
               (MORE)

                    OLMEC (CONT'D)
          In times past, a thousand-man army
          could barely fight its way through
          that cursed forest.

                    CONAN
               (feeling a bruised arm)
          I wouldn't say unscathed.

Conan grabs the chalice of wine and chugs it and then holds
it out to Techotl who gladly refills it.

                    CONAN
               (matter-of-factly)
          We met a creature larger than any
          elephant I've ever seen, but we
          killed it... and except for a few
          bruises --

Techotl drops the wine vessel! His dusky face pallid. His
dark eyes bulging.

Olmec jumps to his feet in complete amazement and shock!

As one, the loungers gasp in stunned horror as if they had
all been punched simultaneously below the belt with their
eyes closed.

Several of them fall to their knees unable to support the
disclosure.

Only Tascela appears unaffected.

Conan glowers about, baffled at their unexpected reaction.

                    CONAN
          By Crom! Have you all gone mad!

Techotl points a shaky finger at Conan.

                    TECHOTL
               (stutters)
          You've slain... the dragon-god?

                    CONAN
               (amused)
          A god, nothing. I killed a foul-
          smelling dragon that would have
          eaten us up if we'd given him the
          opportunity.
               (looks at Valeria; grins)
          And that, we didn't do.

Valeria replies with a guarded smile.

Olmec explodes with a mixture of anger and disbelief in his bellowing voice.

> OLMEC
> That's impossible! Dragons cannot
> die... they're immortal and can
> only kill each other. No man can
> kill them!

> CONAN
> Just within the forest lies its
> carcass, rotting under a tree. Go
> and see for yourselves, if you
> doubt my words.

> OLMEC
> But how could you?! Not even the
> 1000 men who fought through the
> forest to Xuchotl, fifty years ago,
> could kill them... all their
> weapons were useless against their
> armor!

Conan replies with a stuffed mouth, juices flowing from the corners.

> CONAN
> If they would have smeared the tips
> of their arrows and spears with the
> poisonous juice of Derketa's Apples
> and jabbed them in the eyes or
> inside the mouth, they would have
> killed them all. That's how we
> killed it -- but they didn't know,
> did they?

Olmec shakes his head, marveling at Conan's explanation.

> OLMEC
> Many were eaten and killed before
> they were able to reach the safety
> of the city. It's because of the
> dragons that my people remained
> here in Xuchotl after crossing
> over... there was no going back --
> not through that hell.

> VALERIA
> If your people didn't build this
> city, who did?

> OLMEC
> It was built long ago by the once
> powerful race of Kosala.
> (MORE)

                    OLMEC (CONT'D)
          Yet, no one knows its true age...
          not even the base souls that were
          living in Xuchotl when my people
          stumbled upon her.

                    CONAN
          I've seen your type before... by
          the shores of Lake Zuad.
          Tlazitlans?

Olmec, with his calm demeanor back in tow, takes his seat
beside Tascela.

                    OLMEC
          Yes, that is our people. Over
          fifty years ago one of the tribes
          rebelled against the Stygian
          king... but they did not succeed...

FLASHBACK - EXT. SAVANNA - DAY

                    OLMEC (V.O.)
          ... And after their great loss, the
          entire tribe retreated south for
          many weeks.

A leading vanguard of five-hundred Tlazitlan warriors,
followed by old men, women and children make haste carrying
everything with them. Oxen pulling carts and a score of
horses with other domesticated animals, make up the desperate
march southward with a rear guard of five-hundred more
warriors.

EXT. DESERT - DAY

The dead, the dying and the weak litter the rear of the
columns. Collapsed oxen still yoked to the carts are left
dying or dead -- desert flies buzzing about them.

Ruffling vultures land upon the dead while others create a
dark circle of foul feathers huddling around the lifeless --
fighting and fussing for the best portions of the carrion.

EXT. FOREST - DAY

                    OLMEC (V.O.)
          Then the unfortunates entered the
          great forest and were instantly
          beset upon by the terrible dragons!
          They were torn and ripped to
          pieces!

The recovered Tlazitlans trudge through the great forest and as soon as they pass the pool of water the sounds of horrendous screams and roars stop the tribe stone-still in their tracks, the edgy warriors looking every which way for the source of those awful sounds.

A huge, grotesque, and reptilian head pops into view from the forest foliage. Dead eyes stare mercilessly at the Tlazitlans who, although horrified, give the alarm.

Several more gigantic, reptilian heads break into view and like a sudden violent storm, the hounds of hell are turned loose.

The foremost warriors are chomped and gulped immediately by the charging dragons.

Spears and arrows fly -- mixing with the roars of the dragons, the yells of the warriors and the screams of the women and children -- only to be deflected by the impregnable scales.

As the dragons wreak havoc and bodies are trampled and hurled through the air, the warriors unite and create a gauntlet of flight for the others to race through towards the south. Many of the brave warrior are killed and eaten. Their bodies the only shield for the others.

Two dragons fight over a screaming warrior. One gets a leg, the other gets the rest.

One of the few remaining horses gets its head snapped off by one dragon, while the headless body is set upon by another biting off huge chunks of flesh from the quivering beast.

Three warriors try to hold a dragon at bay. Two are quickly snatched up by powerful jaws and the other is trampled by the same creature's stout, short legs.

While the dead and dying are being fed upon by most of the dragons the tribe races through the forest with the rear guard suffering heavy casualties by a single chasing dragon.

But soon that dragon too is finally pacified by a handful of warriors and ceases the chase, to feed.

EXT. PLAIN - DAY

                    OLMEC (V.O.)
          Once past the forest, they found
          themselves facing Xuchotl in the
          distance.

The Tlazitlans make haste towards the city disorganized and
in disarray constantly castings crazed, fearful glances
behind them for fear of pursuit.

The wounded, aided by others, follow more slowly with a small
contingent of warriors bringing up the rear.

EXT. XUCHOTL - NIGHT

                    OLMEC (V.O.)
          But in the plain they had nothing
          to fear from the dragons. For
          theses devils never left the forest
          and were always fighting each
          other. But that was soon to
          change.

Many campfires are lit before the city of Xuchotl with the
Tlazitlans gathered about them.

The night air carries the mourning of women and children and
the horrendous and terrifying roars of the raging monsters
within the forest.

Fear hangs on the fire-lit faces of even the stoutest
warriors around the campfires.

EXT. FOREST - NIGHT

Gaping jaws and snarling snouts.

A pair of roaring dragons engage in a brutal battle. Like
two huge rams, their heads crash together sending one to
ground.

The standing beast rushes in for the kill and clamps down its
massive jaws around the other's long neck only to be met by
thick scales.

The fallen one struggles onto its short, fat legs and shakes
its long and powerful neck causing the other's teeth to lose
their grip and come skidding down and off the neck sparking
the night like flint on steel.

They separate like two boxers gasping for air, tired but
determined, staring at each other with their huge, malevolent
eyes all the while growling, puffing and roaring, their scale
armored bodies suffering little if any damage.

Like two colossal bulls, they bellow, lower their heads, paw
the ground, and charge!

EXT. XUCHOTL - DAY

                    OLMEC (V.O.)
          The city dwellers kept the gates
          closed and tried to persuade them
          to leave.

Bows twang and arrows fly from the battlements of Xuchotl.

The Tlazitlan warriors use their shields to ward off the
arrows and the rest do their best to avoid the volley.

Some take cover behind large cactus plants, others behind the
warriors, while some manage to dodge the shafts in the nick
of time, and some are just not lucky, and get tagged.

Then the flights of arrows cease.

The Tlazitlans slowly look upwards but the archers are gone.

                    OLMEC (V.O.)
          But where could they go? They were
          imprisoned by the forest walls
          surrounding the plain.

A protruding arrowhead is broken and the shaft is removed
from a warrior's shoulder, a few dead bodies are dragged
away, and one warrior surveys his shield needled with arrows.

                    OLMEC (V.O.)
          No, they could not leave. For they
          dared not retrace their steps
          through the forest -- to do so
          would have been madness!

BACK TO PRESENT

                    OLMEC
               (eyes ablaze)
          That night they were visited by a
          man named Tolkemec!

The loungers become aroused with a sense of sudden hatred
whispering pejoratives, with some going as far as to spit at
the mentioned name.

Valeria, leaning back, listens attentively, her repast
complete.

Not so Conan, who listens but is not yet finished eating and
drinking.

> OLMEC
> He was a Tlazitlan... who had
> wandered through the forest with
> many warriors, long ago. He alone
> survived the dragons and was taken
> as a slave within Xuchotl.

FLASHBACK - EXT. XUCHOTL - NORTHERN GATE - NIGHT

The front gate cracks open to a narrow slit from which a
furtive figure sneaks out.

It stops and cautious eyes cast about its immediate
surroundings.

It then sets those cunning eyes upon the campfires before the
great wall of Xuchotl, bunched together like fireflies.

EXT. XUCHOTL - TLAZITLAN CAMP - NIGHT

Around one crackling campfire, warriors with women and
children eat their meager fare.

Out of the darkness a man is suddenly before them.

His hair, interspersed with gray, is lank like theirs but
pinned back by a silver circlet and dressed in a white linen
tunic girded by a simple leather belt, his feet shod with
leather sandals.

The startled warriors at once grab their weapons and quickly
surround the intruder with a circle of spear tips gleaming
like candles from the light of the dancing fire.

A warrior directs his eyes towards one of the women.

> WARRIOR 1
> Bring Tecuhltli and Xotalanc and
> tell them we have a prisoner!

The woman drops everything and rushes away to do as she is
bid.

> TOLKEMEC
> Fear not. I am not your enemy; in
> fact, I've come to help you.

The warriors are surprised to hear him speak their language.

> WARRIOR 2
> (moves spear tip to
> Tolkemec's throat)
> (MORE)

> WARRIOR 2 (CONT'D)
> Who are you that can speak our
> tongue in a city where we have
> never been?!

Two men, TECUHLTLI and XOTALANC, come jogging into the
campfire with the messenger behind them. Both appear similar
in face and figure.

> TECUHLTLI
> Yes, who are you?!

> TOLKEMEC
> Please, let us sit... and I will
> tell you who I am and more.

The two men look at each other and perceiving no danger,
Xotalanc nods at the warriors and dropping their guard they
all take a seat.

Once seated around the campfire, TOLKEMEC looks from one to
the other and sensing their impatience...

> TOLKEMEC
> (smiling lightly)
> My name is Tolkemec and am of your
> race... that is how I know your
> language -- our language.

There's a moment of closer inspection from the group and
heads begin to nod as they discover that his claim is true.

> TECHULTLI
> (suspicious)
> And why are you here? To join us
> or to betray us?

> TOLKEMEC
> May I know with whom I speak?

> TECUHLTLI
> I am Tecuhltli and this is my
> brother, Xotalanc... together we
> lead our people.

> TOLKEMEC
> (raises an eyebrow)
> Ah, two brother chieftains!
> Excellent! Brave warriors,
> betrayal is not on my mind... only
> revenge. My proposal is simple and
> I think fair.

He looks from one brother to the other to gage their interest
and satisfied, continues.

                    TOLKEMEC
          I offer you the city of Xuchotl and
          all I ask in return, is the head of
          every captive.

                    TECUHLTLI
          A strange request.

                    XOTALANC
               (to Tecuhltli)
          Agreed.
               (to Tolkemec)
          Why would you willing betray them
          into our hands?
               (spreading out both hands)
          To people you don't even know.

                    TOLKEMEC
          Does it matter? Why should I not?
          Are we not of the same blood?

Tolkemec turns his gaze towards the campfire for moment his
mind gazing into his past.

                    TOLKEMEC
          Please understand, I am a slave
          among them and my treatment at
          their hands is... less than cordial
          even on a good day.

                    TECUHLTLI
          You seem healthy enough.

Some of warriors grin at the observation.

                    TOLKEMEC
          Aye, but you know not the Kosalans
          as I have come to know them through
          long years of servitude. The body
          is not the only thing susceptible
          under their yoke.

                    XOTALANC
          We've never heard of such people.

                    TOLKEMEC
          Neither had I until I found myself
          under their power. The Kosalans
          are not from this land. They are a
          mysterious people from a land far
          to the east and long ago they were
          driven from their kingdom of Kosala
          by peoples from the south. And
          striking west...

FLASHBACK MONTAGE - THE FOUNDING OF XUCHOTL

1) Native huts dot the plain as far as the eye can see. Black women are preparing the day's meal with the children at play near them. Men are out cultivating the fields and others are returning from the hunt bearing animals hanging from poles between them.

2) A host of Kosalans suddenly appears on the fringe of the plain and the conquest and enslavement of the blacks ensues.

3) Herds of elephants and other beasts of burden, carrying building materials, marble, lapis lazuli, jade, gold, silver and copper, trudge back and forth. Cruel taskmasters flog the black slaves mercilessly.

4) Layer by layer Xuchotl becomes reality until the great city is finally completed, its domes and towers gleaming in the sunlight.

6) The slaves are rounded up and executed.

7) A hunting party of Kosalans finds monstrous bones from the past in the forest.

8) Powerful Kosalan wizards resurrect the dragons turning ancient bones into flesh and use their great magic to bind the creatures within the limits of the forest.

9) The fertile soil throughout the plain is covered with crops.

10) The wizards discover how to grow fruits indoors using the air.

11) The fields and irrigation ditches are abandoned.

BACK TO SCENE

                    TOLKEMEC
          ... For centuries they lived in
          high luxury but in time their
          slothfulness and degenerate ways
          began to eat them away... and now
          they are a weak and dying race
          unfamiliar with sword and magic.

                    TECUHLTLI
          How many?

                         TOLKEMEC
          A few hundred -- but you easily
          outnumber them and more
          importantly, you will wield the
          advantage of surprise.

The two brothers glance at each other looking for any sign of
objection from the other and finding none they turn their
attention back to Tolkemec.

                         TECHULTLI
          Into the forest we dare not return
          and on the plain we cannot
          remain... we have no choice but to
          trust you -- but betray us....

                         TOLKEMEC
          Fear not, my word is true. If you
          are betrayed it will not be by my
          hand. My reward will be the
          captives -- will they be mine?

                         XOTALANC
               (puzzled)
          For what purpose?

                         TOLKEMEC
          That is my concern. Your concern
          is to win the city. Do we have a
          pact?

Tecuhltli considers him still mystified, yet nods.

                         TOLKEMEC
          Excellent!

                         TECUHLTLI
          Now you. How will you get us
          within the walls?

                         TOLKEMEC
          The great gate before you will be
          left open at dawn. Be ready!

BACK TO PRESENT

                         OLMEC
          Dawn came and the halls of Xuchotl
          ran red with blood. Nearly a 100
          captives were taken and these were
          given into the hands of Tolkemec.

Olmec turns his face to one of his subjects.

                         OLMEC
          Wine!

A woman, SOLESA, hurries to a well provisioned table near her
and fills a chalice for her prince.

Moving carefully, so as not to spill its contents, she bows
before him and serves him the wine cup. She then bows out
and moves quickly beside the sitting giant and one step back.

Olmec drains the cup in one gulp.

                         OLMEC
                    That night, cries of unimaginable
                    pain filled the city of Xuchotl.
                    For many nights following, Tolkemec
                    tortured and killed the wretched
                    captives who had fallen into his
                    power.

Olmec looks up at the girl and she refills the wine cup.

Olmec's dark, forboding eyes stare inside the cup as if
looking for a sign. The wistful thought vanishes and the
bull of a man takes an easy sip of the red wine.

The Tlazitlans, littered about the great throne room, listen
listlessly as Olmec continues with a passionless voice.

                         OLMEC
                    For several years thereafter, peace
                    reigned throughout the city ruled
                    by the two brothers and Tolkemec
                    who soon took a wife from among
                    them. Tolkemec taught them the
                    secret of growing fruit within the
                    city by use of air. Not only was
                    this knowledge opportune, but
                    fortunate. For with the killing of
                    the Kosalans, the spell that had
                    bound the dragons to the forest had
                    been broken and at night the beasts
                    would roar and ram the walls and
                    fight amongst each other spilling
                    much blood upon the plain and that
                    is when --

Conan and Valeria note the self-censorship and, while Olmec
takes a swig of wine to cover it, Valeria nudges Conan's boot
with her own beneath the ornate, ivory table and watches with
the corner of her eye as Conan acknowledges with a subtle
nod.

                    OLMEC
          And thus they remained inside these
          walls feasting, loving and raising
          their children.

Olmec's dark eyes rest for a moment upon the exotic beauty,
Tascela.

                    OLMEC
          But because of a woman, it did not
          last.

FLASHBACK - INT. XUCHOTL - GREAT THRONE ROOM - DAY

                    OLMEC (V.O.)
          There was a woman that both
          brothers and Tolkemec craved.

Beneath one of the skylights, Xotalanc stands amidst a large
gathering and facing him is his bride, Tascela!

An ancient, lightly straps together their right hands, with a
long strip of purple silk.

He then places his hand over theirs, utters a few indistinct
words, pulls the strip of purple silk until it unwinds from
their hands, lets it drop to the floor and the marriage
ceremony is over.

Those around them cheer and shout for joy as the couple
embraces.

Tolkemec celebrates with the crowd but his eyes betray his
heart for want of Tascela.

Tecuhltli stands as if alone. He is deaf to the sounds of
the joyous gathering. There is no smile upon his lips nor
any mark of jubilation on his features; instead, he battles
to mask his great resentment and burning jealousy.

INT. XUCHOTL - FOURTH FLOOR - TASCELA'S CHAMBER - NIGHT

                    OLMEC (V.O.)
          But marriage was not enough to cut
          off Tecuhltli's maddening desire.

The glowing fire-stones highlight the beauty of Tascela as
she sleeps soundly in an ivory bed upon plush pillows, her
lithe figure wrapped in a gossamer robe.

The pulsing, fiery light emanating from the tiles surrounds the bed in a surreal fringing glow and keeps time with the gentle rise and fall of her inviting breasts.

From the darker shadows of the chamber, Tecuhltli emerges to gaze upon the irresistible woman lying in slumber.

Gently, Tecuhltli slides his eager arms under her warm breathing body and lifts her up against his chest.

Tascela awakens with a soft gasp, but her dark eyes and blood-red lips smile as she realizes who it is and what is transpiring.

Tecuhltli sneaks out of the chamber with his prize, her arms wrapped around his neck.

BACK TO PRESENT

                    OLMEC
          Xotalanc was enraged and the
          council of the tribe was called.

FLASHBACK - INT. XUCHOTL - FOURTH FLOOR - GREAT CHAMBER - DAY

Underneath the lapis lazuli ceiling pecked with countless dormant fire-stones, an almost empty chamber echoes with the indistinct voices of people trickling in.

The tribal council of five ancients sits upon marble seats behind a long and narrow matching rectangular table.

The room is bare of any other chairs or tables. No tapestries on the surrounding chalcedony walls. No rugs on the dim vacillating tiles. No ostentatious decoration of any kind.

INT. XUCHOTL - FOURTH FLOOR - GREAT CHAMBER - LATER (MOS)

In a crowded chamber, Xotalanc stands before the council and accuses his brother vehemently and then points to his wife who stands alone at one end of the table silently.

AN HOUR LATER

The five ancients finish their hushed deliberations with Tascela standing before them, Xotalanc standing at one end of the table and Tecuhltli standing at the other end. Behind the three facing the council, the chamber is packed tight.

The leader of the council faces the woman, brushes the perspiration from his forehead and then asks Tascela a question. Tascela, acting swiftly and without hesitation, points to Tecuhltli!

Xotalanc explodes and his retainers rush in to hold him down.

>   OLMEC (V.O.)
> Fearing to make a decision, the
> council had allowed Tascela to
> choose between the two. After that
> fateful day, Xuchotl became hell.

MONTAGE - BLOOD FEUD

1) A bloodbath ensues in the Great Hall between the forces of Xotalanc and those of Tecuhltli. Great amounts of blood cover the floor, making it almost impossible to discern the pulsating molten tiles.

2) A headless corpse gushes as Tecuhltli and Tolkemec overwhelm the forces of Xotalanc in the Halls of Silence. Xotalanc makes a desperate and hasty retreat.

>   OLMEC (V.O.)
> Tolkemec played no loyalty. He
> would switch between the two
> brothers on a whim, when it served
> his purpose.

3) Xotalanc and Tolkemec break into Tecuhltli's fortress and a bitter, bloody battle commences. Warriors slip on the bloody, throbbing tiles and are instantly hacked to death. Eyes are punctured with daggers. Shoulders, hands and feet are hacked off.

4) In a dark hall of the lower levels illuminated only by the weird glow of green and red-orange, a terrific battle rages. Screams, cries and yells mix with the clang and clash of swords and daggers.

5) Three of Tecuhltli's men are ambushed on a winding ivory staircase by a large sortie led by Xotalanc. No way up or down.

6) Xotalanc's men dump the remains of the three caught on the staircase, amid yells of delight, on Eagles's Way before the great bronze door. Two are dismembered and one flayed -- minus their heads.

BACK TO PRESENT

Valeria winces in utter disgust at the diabolical cruelty of
the feud and even Conan grimaces and grunts at the magnitude
of the atrocities painted before them by Olmec.

> OLMEC
> The city, as you are aware, is oval
> in design and the three warring
> clans took up fortified strongholds
> in different quarters. Xotalanc
> took the eastern quarter, we the
> western quarter and Tolkemec the
> southern portion of the city -- but
> he, was not a man but a devil...
> far worse than Xotalanc.

Olmec gives the wine cup to the girl and dismisses her.
Then, looking directly at Techotl who's standing a step back
behind the two guests, he makes an upward motion with his
chin and Techotl quickly removes the cups and vessels from
the table and limps lightly towards the lounging area.

> OLMEC
> Xotalanc's vengeance was
> understandable. He had lost his
> woman. But Tolkemec was a dark
> fiend... filled with the knowledge
> of ancients long past... pilfered
> from the tombs of the catacombs...

IN SLOW MOTION

Olmec's voice sounds far away and indistinct as Valeria
shifts her eyes from him to find Tascela's disquieting stare
fixated upon her.

Tascela's face is bereft of all emotion or care like a
beautiful marble slab, cold and soulless.

Valeria breaks free of the silent beauty's boring gaze, her
eyes returning to the seated prince.

BACK TO NORMAL SPEED

Olmec's eyes light up with pride as he begins to recall a
distant memory, the crescendo of his voice rising in ecstasy.

                    OLMEC
          ... But twelve years ago during a
          night raid we surprised them with
          their gate still open and they
          paid!

FLASHBACK - INT. XUCHOTL - TOLKEMEC'S WAY - NIGHT

Like two colliding waves, the forces of Tecuhltli and
Tolkemec come crashing between the brilliant green fire and
the dancing flames beneath their sandal shod feet.

The forces of Tolkemec and Tecuhltli are evenly matched as
they battle savagely, until Olmec crashes through their line
and turns the tide.

The reserves from the Tolkemec fortress charge out to staunch
the onslaught but find themselves beaten back into the
fortress and begin to fall under the sword.

SERIES OF SHOTS - TOLKEMEC'S CAPTURE AND TORTURE

1) Olmec and his warriors enter their enemy's fortress and
put every man, woman, and child to the sword.

2) Tolkemec is cornered and taken captive.

3) Upsidedown and spread-eagle by chains, Tolkemec is
tortured mercilessly. His painful cries of agony fill the
Halls of Silence.

4) Barely alive and looking more like a corpse, Tolkemec is
thrown into a cell in the dungeon.

5) The cell door opens and the warriors are struck dumb by
what they find. Tolkemec is gone!

BACK TO PRESENT

                    OLMEC
          ... But Tolkemec escaped into the
          catacombs where he died, for we
          never saw him again. But some say
          he still lives among the dead,
          howling and hungering for
          vengeance. Yet because of that
          woman, the feud continues to this
          day and except for Tascela, all of
          us were born into it... and it will
          kill every one of us in the end.
                    (MORE)

                    OLMEC (CONT'D)
          There were a great many of us in
          the beginning, but look around you.

Conan and Valeria sweep the chamber with their eyes.

                    OLMEC
          That is all that remains of the
          Tecuhltli clan.
               (shaking head)
          The Xotalancas cannot number much
          more. Our women have not born any
          children for fifteen years and we
          have seen none among our enemy.
          Like the Kosalans, our end is near.
          And no one has ever left this city
          except for --

Valeria raises an eyebrow and Conan squints just a tad at
Olmec's second self-check.

                    OLMEC
          Yet we dare not! For over fifty
          years none has dared for we are not
          accustomed to the heat of day nor
          to the physical demands you face
          outside of Xuchotl. Even if there
          were no dragons we would not last.

Conan rises up from the table followed by Valeria.

                    CONAN
          Well, dragons or not, we're
          leaving. Besides, this blood feud
          of yours is no concern of ours.
          So, if you'll let Techotl guide us
          to one of the gates, we'll take our
          leave.

Tascela's eyes become imperious and her tapered fingers roll
up into fists. Her lips part but Olmec rests a massive hand
on her arm to stop her utterance.

                    OLMEC
          The sun has fallen and night will
          soon be upon us. Would it be wise
          to travel the plain during the
          night?

Conan unfazed, shrugs his huge, wide shoulders.

                    CONAN
          Why not? We slept in the plain
          last night without sight or sound
          of them.

A dread smile spreads across Tascela's countenance.

                    TASCELA/REGAL WOMAN
          You'd risk leaving Xuchotl?!

Conan's smouldering blue-eyes regard her unfavorably, but
Tascela not so much as glances at him, her gaze fully on
Valeria.

Without looking at Tascela, Olmec intervenes.

                    OLMEC
          That, they would. But why leave
          now? Why not join us?! Fight with
          us against the Xotalancas and you
          will be well rewarded. You are
          warriors by profession and we have
          great wealth in jewels, silver and
          gold. Help us destroy the
          Xotalancas and you'll have all the
          treasure you can carry.

Valeria with one hand resting on the curve of her hip and the
other playing idly with the pommel of her sword...

                    VALERIA
          And the dragons? Will you help us?
          Now that you know, killing them
          with archers will be easy.

                    OLMEC
          That we can do -- only, after years
          of close-quarter fighting we have
          forgotten the use of the bow. But
          it matters not. It would not take
          us long to relearn the use of the
          bow.

Valeria glances up at Conan.

                    VALERIA
          It's as good a job as any, no? I'm
          willing, if you are.

                    CONAN
            (grinning)
          We're broker than a dead man's
          bones and since killing is our
          trade....

                    OLMEC
          We are agreed then?!

Conan pulls his eyes away from the smiling girl and nods.

                         CONAN
              Now, where can we sleep so we can
              be rested for tomorrow's slaughter?

Techotl is beside himself with joy at the fortuitous outcome.

                         OLMEC
              Techotl! Solesa! Attend to their
              needs.

Conan and Valeria are escorted by Techotl and Solesa
respectively towards a door left of the dais.

As they follow their guides towards the door, the two
mercenaries pause and turn at the sound of pounding.

Behind the throne, five red nails are being hammered into the
shiny, ebony pillar.

Valeria catches a glimpse of Olmec with his chin on his huge
fist, his eyes burning with a strange light and Tascela
leaning back on her seat speaking to her morose, lady-in-
waiting, Yasala.

Yasala is bent over her mistress's shoulder with her ear to
Tascela's lips taking in every whispered word.

INT. TECUHLTLI - EAGLE'S TIER - HALL - EVENING

Down a long narrow corridor they move, the eerie, fulgent
glow of emerald fire-stones and burning, pulsing floor tiles
combining to light the way.

Solesa stops before a door, opens it, enters and motions for
Valeria to follow.

Valeria enters but turns around within the door frame and
leans back against the jamb with her arms crossed over her
chest.

                         CONAN
              (scowls; to Techotl)
              Eh, what's the idea? Where's my
              bed?

                         TECHOTL
              (pointing)
              Your chamber is over there.

Conan looks and sees a chamber door across the hall, that's
one door down.

Techotl eases himself towards the indicated door.

Conan's eyes follow him for just a moment and then they
return back to Valeria with an annoyed stare.

Valeria, her feminine, voluptuous figure now framed by the
doorway and with a wonderful hip thrown to one side and one
hand resting on it, smiles vindictively and slowly shuts him
out with the door in his face.

Conan growls under his breath.

                    CONAN
          Damn wenches! They're all the same!

Conan follows after Techotl, irked at having missed his
gazelle.

INT. CONAN'S CHAMBER - EVENING

Conan's roaming eyes take in the ornate room and look up at
the rectangular skylights embedded within the ceiling through
which he can see stars beginning to light the darkening sky.

Still looking up, Conan muses.

                    CONAN
               You know, if I were a Xotalanc, I
               would break through those
               skylights.
                    (puzzled; looks at
                     Techotl)
               Why don't they?

                    TECHOTL
                    (shaking head)
               It would be a waste of time to
               attempt it. Xuchotl is covered
               with many towers, domes and steep
               roofs making it very difficult to
               climb -- but even if they could,
               the skylights are unbreakable.

Conan sits down on the edge of a wide jade bed and begins to
unbuckle his broadsword.

                    TECHOTL
               You see, Tecuhltli is a fortress
               made so by the feud... all four
               floors and even the catacombs
               underneath Tecuhltli have been
               carefully fortified against an
               attack.
                    (MORE)

                    TECHOTL (CONT'D)
          This floor, the highest, is called
          the Eagle's Tier, the third floor
          is called the Ape's Tier, the
          second is the Tiger's Tier and the
          last one is known as the Serpent's
          Tier. Every chamber, hallway, and
          staircase throughout the city of
          Xuchotl has a name.

Conan stands to his full height and stretches his long and
powerful arms over his head and yawns.

                    CONAN
          Who is she?

Techotl stares at him unsure of what he's asking.

                    CONAN
          Tascela. Is she Olmec's wife?

Techotl shivers with fright and putting a finger to his
trembling lips, closes the door.

                    TECHOTL
          She is not his wife. Tascela is
          the reason for the feud.

Conan's eyebrows meet in confusion.

                    CONAN
          What?! Make sense, man.

                    TECHOTL
          Tascela was Xotalanc's wife. She
          is the woman that was stolen by
          Tecuhltli. It is because of her
          that we have been fighting all this
          time.

Conan stares at him as if he's insane but Techotl is dead
serious.

                    TECHOTL
               (in a subdued voice)
          Yes! It is her! Believe me when I
          tell you that Tascela is that
          woman.

                    CONAN
               (incredulous)
          Are you trying to tell me that
          beautiful young woman was
          Xotalanc's wife?!

Techotl nods his head feverishly.

                    TECHOTL
          Yes! But there's more. She was
          the reason that the two brothers
          fought against the king of Stygia.
          The king had sought to make her his
          own.

Conan blinks his eyes, incredulous at what he's hearing.

                    TECHOTL
          The woman is a witch! She has the
          secret knowledge and power of
          everlasting youth.

                    CONAN
          What secret?

Techotl shakes his head like a nervous rattler.

                    TECHOTL
          I dare not say! But know this, it
          is a black foulness that stains the
          entire city of Xuchotl.

Conan is about to ask him another question but Techotl
cautions him to silence, opens the chamber door and sliding
out and closes the door behind him.

INT. VALERIA'S CHAMBER - EVENING

A sheathed sword is tossed onto a couch.

Valeria examines the chamber while she rebuckles her belt.
Two bolted doors are right and left of the room and opposite
the entrance, a bolted copper-bound door.

                    VALERIA
          Where do these doors lead?

Solesa, using both hands, indicates the right and left doors.

                    SOLESA
          These two doors lead to connecting
          chambers.
                    (indicates copper-bound
                     door)
          And this one opens to a corridor at
          the end of which is another door
          which opens into a staircase that
          leads down to the catacombs.
                    (MORE)

                    SOLESA (CONT'D)
          But you have nothing to fear... you
          are safe.

                    VALERIA
               (retorts)
          Fear? Not likely. I just want to
          know where I've docked -- and I
          don't need you sleeping at the foot
          of my couch... I don't like it --
          not from women. I prefer to be
          alone.

Valeria flicks her head back towards the door they entered.

Without a word, Solesa leaves the chamber.

After the door closes, Valeria throws the bolts on the doors,
sits on the edge of a carnelian divan, pulls off her soft
leather boots and swinging her legs onto the couch, stretches
them out.

As she sinks back into the plush pillows, a malicious smile
plays on her full lips as she thinks about the Cimmerian.

VALERIA'S IMAGINATION - INT. CONAN'S CHAMBER - NIGHT

Conan lies on his bed with his hands behind his black mane
scowling at the emerald, fire-stone encrusted ceiling as
silent pejoratives escape his lips.

BACK TO SCENE

Valeria's beautiful smile widens as she laughs silently under
her breath.

She nestles her full, lithe figure comfortably into the
couch, takes a deep breath lifting her generous bosom high
and as it falls, with a light smile still playing on the
corners of her lips, she closes her eyes.

EXT. XUCHOTL - DEAD OF NIGHT

A wicked wind howls through a black night jetting like a
vengeful soul between the domes, turrets, and towers that
thrust up against the starry sky like silent giant monoliths.

INT. XUCHOTL - FOURTH FLOOR - NARROW HALL - NIGHT

A ghostly green mist fills the confines of a corridor as
stealthy figures slink along the uncanny magma river beneath
silent feet.

DREAM - INT. VALERIA'S CHAMBER - NIGHT

Valeria awakens abruptly in a nebulous, emerald glow.

Above her hovers a pulsating, humongous black blossom covered
in dew that seems to block out the entire ceiling.

The blossom's dew reflects the sinister green light, as if
jeweled with countless, brilliant emeralds.

From the black blossom, dark twisting streams issue forth and
envelope her face with a sense of blissful tranquility.

Valeria's eyelids become heavy and half close as she succumbs
to the exotic scent of the blossom. A grateful smile
accentuates her lovely cheeks as her eyes fully close under
the black spell.

A single pear-shaped dewdrop hangs from one of the petals and
with the pulsation of the blossom, the invisible thread is
cut.

IN SLOW MOTION

The glittering emerald splashes lightly on one of her
enraptured cheeks.

INT. VALERIA'S CHAMBER - NIGHT

Valeria is jolted cruelly into a state of full wakefulness.

Instead of a giant black blossom pulsing above her, she finds
a woman.

Valeria's face snarls.

The woman attempts to flee but Valeria, enraged and endowed
with reflexes of a cat, pounces on her catching her roughly
by an arm.

The girl struggles and fights viciously trying to break free.
She throws a wild swing and Valeria ducks and is quickly
behind the woman with her right arm across her throat
immobilizing her.

Valeria, with a dark smile on her face, then forces the
woman's left arm mercilessly up behind her back until she
cries out in submission.

Valeria, a head taller, whips the woman around and grabs her
chin with a strong hand to have a look at her. It's Yasala!

                    VALERIA
          What the hell were you doing
          standing over me?

Yasala remains silent, but Valeria's sharp eyes catch a large
silhouetted item on the pulsing floor.

                    VALERIA
          Pick it up!

Valeria grabs a chunk of the woman's hair and shoves her to
the floor beside it.

Yasala looks back at Valeria's deadly eyes before taking hold
of the it.

With a large blossom in hand she stands before her captor.

Valeria snatches it from her, puzzled at the black blossom
the size of a woman's head with a long green stem. Her eyes
narrow as she realizes what it is.

                    VALERIA
          The black lotus! The blossom of
          deep sleep. One of these petals
          must have touched my cheek... if I
          had not awakened -- you tried to
          drug me! Why?!

But Yasala only stares at her in stubborn silence, her morose
features ever her manner.

Valeria spins her around and violently takes hold of her
locks and twists Yasala's arm behind her back again forcing
her to her knees. Valeria then begins to ratchet the arm
upwards.

                    VALERIA
          Tell me, wench! Or I'll rip your
          arm out. By Mitra, I will!

Yasala gasps and grimaces, her body struggling to break free,
but the only reply she gives is an unyielding shake of her
head.

Valeria explodes.

                         VALERIA
                    You court slut!

Valeria kicks Yasala between her shoulders with the bottom of
her barefoot, sending the woman sprawling across the floor.

Valeria glowers at the woman with eyes afire.

As the fallen girl upturns her sulky but attractive face,
she's met by those blazing eyes.

Yasala's large dark eyes mirror the weird, emerald green,
like those of a night creature.

Valeria, uneasy in the bolted pin, shifts her eyes about and
angles her head to listen but is rewarded only by a dead
silence that rests within and without the chamber like a
black pall on a coffin.

Valeria strides over, crouches down beside the girl and pulls
her head back by the hair, Valeria's face only inches from
the girl's downcast eyes.

                         VALERIA
                    Why drug me?

Yasala lifts her eyes and stares at her defiant and laconic.

                         VALERIA
                     (boiling over)
                    Why put me under its spell?! You
                    vile, piece of -- who sent you?!
                    Tascela?

Yasala drops her gaze refusing to answer.

Valeria viciously slaps her left cheek with her open right
palm and backhands her other cheek on the way back. The
slaps resound distinctly in the soundless room.

                         VALERIA
                     (in a low, unforgiving
                      voice)
                    By Mitra, you will talk or I'll
                    whip you into hell.

Valeria drags the girl by the hair towards the canopied bed
with long, heavy silken cords dangling round about it, like a
veil.

She releases the girl at her feet and yanks several of the
hanging cords, like hair from a scalp, and ties several of
them together to create a whip.

She pulls two more of the long cords from their moorings and looks down at Yasala.

                    VALERIA
          Soon, you will tell me everything.

                                        FADE TO BLACK:

Swift, crisp snaps land on flesh again and again.

Quick painful gasps, low moans and whimpers struggle to restrain from crying out or screaming.

INT. VALERIA'S CHAMBER - NIGHT

Fiery, emerald cat-eyes clustered and spread throughout the ceiling, watch the tableau below.

Yasala lies facedown on the couch. Her wrists and ankles are bound and secured to a couch leg on each end by taut cords.

The glow of the pulsing floor tiles reach up to mix with the eerie green light from above providing more than ample illumination in the for-the-moment torture chamber.

Her fine tunic is torn open down to her lower back and many welts and stripes cover her dark skin including her legs.

Yasala bites her lower lip drawing blood, as another blow from the impromptu whip strikes her lashed tender flesh and her entire body quivers uncontrollably as if electrified.

Valeria, her forehead glistening with sweat and her golden locks moist, flails her mercilessly until bringing her strong arm back for another strike, she hears a reluctant plea.

                    YASALA
          (in a low, moaning voice)
          Mercy! Please, no more. I'll
          speak -- I'll tell you everything.

Valeria throws back her locks with a quick movement of her golden head and drops down to cut Yasala's ankles and wrists free from the restraining cords and pulls the girl to her feet, but Yasala slumps down onto the couch, her flesh reeling as a portion of her back makes contact with it.

Yasala rises slowly and painfully to a sitting position and raises a shaky hand and points towards a small carnelian table supporting a golden vessel and cups.

                         YASALA
                    (trembling)
               Wine...
                    (grimaces and swallows)
               ... my throat, is parched.

Valeria grabs the vessel and hands it to Yasala who rises to
her feet to take it, her body trembling and somewhat off-
balance.

Valeria watches as she raises the golden vessel to her lips
but instead of quenching her thirst, Yasala hurls the
contents into Valeria's face.

Valeria, caught off-guard, falls back several steps while her
hands work feverishly to wipe away to stinging wine from her
eyes.

Through blurring, stinging pain Valeria manages to see
Yasala, in one quick motion, throw back the bolt and open the
copper-bound door and streak down the hall in a mad flight of
desperation.

In a flash, Valeria dashes after her.

INT. XUCHOTL - EAGLE'S TIER - HALL - NIGHT

Yasala, galvanized by fear and having a head start, rounds
the corner down the hall ahead of her pursuer.

When Valeria finally turns the corner she finds the hall
empty and Yasala, vanished!

Only an open door, at the end of hall, framing a pitch
blackness, greets her searching, angry eyes.

Cautiously Valeria sneaks towards the open door only yards
away.

She peeks within and finds a shaft with a staircase that
disappears straight down into the darkness.

A foul stench assails her and she shudders in repulsion.

Denied and troubled, Valeria half-turns to return when
suddenly she hears a woman's cry struggling upwards as if
from the bottomless pit.

                         YASALA (V.O.)
                    (in abject fear)
               Help! Someone, please help me! In
               Set's name --

A single horrific scream reaches Valeria and as it dies away Valeria hears a wicked snickering, giggling sound that slowly, in its turn, fades away.

Valeria, rattled, does not bother to close the door, but runs back to her room as fast as her bare feet can carry her.

INT. VALERIA'S CHAMBER - NIGHT

Valeria bolts the door behind her, leans her back against it, takes a deep breath and lets it out, brushes her brow and like a cat begins to wipe away the wetness of the wine still remaining on her face and golden locks.

INT. TECUHLTLI - EAGLE'S TIER - GUARDROOM - SAME TIME

Relaxed but alert, two warriors keep watch armed with spears, swords and daggers.

One warrior, XATMEC, 28, stands against the wall with one foot on the floor. The other leg is bent with the flat of the foot planted on the wall. His arms are folded across his chest and his spear, like his back and foot, rests angled against the wall next to him.

KAMETECHOL, 30, sits on a chalcedony bench spinning his spear between his palms as if trying to kindle a fire above the dull, pulsating magma-like floor.

Xatmec glances at his companion for a spell as he spins the spear back and forth.

                    XATMEC
          It is said that tomorrow we attack
          Xotalanc. Olmec, himself, will
          lead us and with the aid of the
          strangers, we will kill many.

Kametechol continues spinning the spear as he ponders the news. After a few moments, he stops the spinning and looks up at Xatmec.

                    KAMETECHOL
          Tell me. What happens if with
          their help we are victorious over
          the remaining Xotalancas?

                    XATMEC
               (grinning)
          You know very well what will
          happen.
                    (MORE)

                         XATMEC (CONT'D)
          Red nails will be driven into the
          Pillar of Vengeance for the dead
          and the prisoners will be
          quartered, flayed and then
          burned... as is our custom.

                         KAMETECHOL
               (troubled)
          That is not what I meant. I meant
          afterwards -- after we've killed
          them all? You and I have fought
          them all our lives. We have hated
          them. We have known nothing else.
          What will be left for us to do?

Xatmec considers Kametechol's burning questions for a brief
moment and then shrugs them off, not worried or caring about
the future.

A sudden, subtle noise outside the great bronze door puts
them on high alert.

                         KAMETECHOL
               (in a subdued voice)
          Quick to the door! I'll take the
          Eye.

Leaving his spear behind, Xatmec carefully slides out his
sword and once at the entrance presses an ear to the bronze
door and listens carefully.

Kametechol peers into the Eye and his jaw drops.

Through the Eye, he sees a thick mob of truculent men and
women before the great bronze door -- dark, hostile visages
with their ears plugged with their fingers or cupped with
their hands.

One, in the middle and forefront of the group and wearing a
headdress of feathers, puts a set of pipes to his lips.

Kametechol pulls away from the Eye swiftly to cry out an
alarm but the shrill, piercing pipes cut off his attempt
trapping the cry in his throat.

The strange, unearthly sound forces Xatmec into a statuesque-
like trance, his ear still glued to the door and his eyes and
mouth open in empty horror.

Further away from the door, Kametechol, though not
immobilized, struggles terrifically with his hands cupped
over his ears to break the hold of the hellish sound
attempting to steal his will and self-control.

His face contorts beyond recognition as he fights the cursed spell and the insupportable, penetrating, painful sound.

In one last, desperate effort, his body shaking with tremendous tension, he lifts up his face towards the countless blazing green-eyes of the ceiling and cries out in a thunderous roar alerting his clan.

Then the fifing rises to a higher deadlier pitch and Xatmec screams, overwhelmed by agony and excruciating pain and like a crazed man he pulls open the door.

IN SLOW MOTION

Several Clansmen stumble into the guardroom and immediately cover their ears at the painful sounds emanating from the Xotalanc leader.

The mind piercing notes suddenly cease and Xatmec free, sees the enemy before him for the first time.

Bravely, Xatmec rushes out, his sword swirling above his head and hatred blazing in his eyes.

A half-dozen swords quickly cut him down and the Xotalanc horde charges into the Tecuhltli fortress with prolonged maniacal war cries echoing throughout the guardroom.

Maddened by pain and by the fall of his friend, Kametechol takes hold of his spear leaning against the wall and manfully confronts the rolling onslaught, spearing the gut of the first Xotalanc.

As members of the Tecuhltli clan flood the chamber behind Kametechol, his belly is torn open by two swords and his head flies from his stationary body.

The two bodies of opposing forces meet with clanging and sparking steel.

Blood spurts and splatters.

INT. TECUHLTLI - STAIRCASE - SAME TIME

Six guards from the lower tiers speed up the stairs with bared swords to join the fray.

INT. VALERIA'S CHAMBER - SAME TIME

Valeria is sitting on the couch pulling on her other boot when the crash of weapons and war cries reach her chamber!

                         VALERIA
                       (annoyed)
                 What the devil is it now?

She hurriedly pulls on the last boot, picks up the sword
belt, rises and as she moves to the door straps it on.

INT. CONAN'S CHAMBER - SAME TIME

Conan's jumps out of bed, agile and alert like an aroused
lion, with sword in hand as the pandemonium of steel on steel
banishes the remaining strings of slumber.

Conan bounds to the door, opens it and looks down the
corridor in time to see an almost out-of-breath Techotl
running towards him, his eyes screaming danger.

                         TECHOTL
                 They are inside! The Xotalancas!

INT. TECUHLTLI - EAGLE'S TIER - HALL - NIGHT

Conan runs out leaving the chamber door open and as he joins
up with Techotl, Valeria enters the hall.

                         VALERIA
                       (agitated)
                 What the hell is all that noise?!

She merges with them in a dogtrot towards the throne room.

                         VALERIA
                 Don't these people ever sleep?

                         CONAN
                 According to our friend here...

Conan quick-glances back at Techotl who's jogging
uncomfortably close behind them.

                         CONAN
                 ... It's the Xotalancas. They've
                 breached the fortress, and by that
                 ruckus, I don't doubt it.

INT. TECUHLTLI - EAGLE'S TIER - GREAT THRONE ROOM - NIGHT

They burst through the door with Conan in the middle.

Before their eyes a savage medley of death plays itself out.

Twenty Xotalancas, men and women, with white skulls on their chests and gray tunics respectively, fight like a hell-eyed devils against their Tecuhltli brethren.

But just as savagely the Tecuhltli with their lank manes moving wildly in the fray, cleave and skewer with ruthless precision.

Bodies from both sides lie all about the throne room, dead or dying especially in hall leading into the throne room.

Over these bodies, the

SIX GUARDS

from below come rampaging in, to partake in the bloodletting feud.

OLMEC

wearing only a loincloth and with a sword to match his size, fights two Xotalancas before the throne and with a great arcing swing, lops off both

HEADS

simultaneously, that fall back into the raging melee behind their headless bodies.

TASCELA

armed with a sword, emerges from one of the two small inner chambers further back, that straddle the pillar of Vengeance and jumps into the fierce fighting slicing and cutting every which way. Tascela's

SWORD ARM

thrusts forward and a

MALE XOTALANC

stiffens as the cross-guard of her sword is stopped by his belly, a good portion of the blade protruding from his back.

Tascela pulls the sword swiftly and easily from the impaled body leaving him standing in place for a moment and then the

MAN

crumbles to the floor.

Between the radiant green eyes above and the dull, red-orange
pulsating tiles below, Tlazitlans, wielding steel, shift back
and forth like a deadly game of tug-of-war.

And as Conan and Valeria crash into the chaotic feud against
the hated enemy, an exultant roar from the Tecuhltli fills
the room as one voice shaking the very foundations of the
throne room -- a veritable bedlam of madness.

The sudden cry of high energy attracts the attention of Olmec
as he pulls his sword from a lifeless Xotalanc, and
discovering its source, sneers with one side of his dark
bearded face.

CONAN

heavier and towering above everyone except Olmec, moves
faster and with more agility than a fighting lion as he hacks
and crushes his opponents with unblockable blows while

VALERIA

eyes afire and her lovely lips parted in a fierce smile,
fights beside the powerful Cimmerian, dazzling and blinding
her opponents with her fast moves and inexorable, confounding
swordplay. A

XOTALANC WARRIOR

shoves his broken sword into the neck of his adversary and
before he is able to pull it out a

BLOOD-HUNGRY WOMAN

cuts him down and then stamps his face with her heel.

CONAN

shatters through a sword and takes the man's shoulder off.

TWO WARRIORS

take the place of the fallen one but before they can engage
him,

CONAN'S LEFT ARM

strikes out like a viper and grabs the throat of one and uses
him as a shield choking the life out of him as his sword
deals with the other. The

MADDENED XOTALANC

lunges but Conan, like a bullfighter, sidesteps leaving the
choking body, like a bullfighter's cape, to receive the
driving sword. The

UNFORTUNATE MAN

screams in death and Conan cleaves the other, the Xotalanc's
sword trapped in the body of the dead man, from the neck down
to the chest.

BLOOD

splatters everywhere!

The last

WOMAN

of Xotalanc, her eyelids fluttering, falls clutching a

DAGGER

in her heart.

Battles move in and out of chambers and halls leading into
the Great Throne Room with undiminished ferocity.

VALERIA

ducks and sweeps her two-edged sword taking off a leg.
Faster and stronger than the average man,

VALERIA

rises, parries a thrust and punches the man full in the face
taking him off his feet and sending him backwards to fall
unconscious upon his back and an

ALLY

swoops down and slices his throat before quickly taking on
another Xotalanc.

Conan's quick, blazing eyes catch a fallen warrior embed his
dagger in Valeria's lower calf but she doesn't notice as she
battles a pressing attacker.

He tries to crawl away and weakly looks up in time to see
Conan's broadsword descend to split his skull wide open.

Soon the throne room is left with only a handful of the
outnumbered Xotalancas fighting against great odds and

MOMENTS LATER

the last one is cut down like a dog by four Tecuhltli.

An eerie wolf-like howl of victory reverberates throughout
the Great Throne Room with swords raised in triumph.

Blood and gore cover the entire room. Tired, haggard, but
gleam-eyed Tecuhltli, covered in the same, take stock of
their wounds.

Tascela canvasses the throne room with narrowed eyes and
finding what she sought, she moves towards it.

She crouches beside the Xotalanc wearing the feathered
headdress and removes the pipes shoved into his waistline
behind his leather belt.

Conan grabs Valeria's arm lightly and she turns to meet his
dark, scarred, blood-covered countenance.

                    CONAN
                  (mutters)
            You're wounded.

Valeria is about to examine her arms but Conan stops her with
a hand and slaps her outer thigh gently with his other to
indicate which leg.

                    CONAN
            Your calf.

Valeria positions her leg for a better look and flinches,
feeling the pain for the first time.

Ignoring the pain she looks the Cimmerian over who's covered
from head to foot in crimson blood, and she laughs good-
naturedly at the sight.

                  VALERIA
       And you, Cimmerian, look as if you
       just crawled out of a pool of
       blood.

Conan grins and shakes a great deal of clinging blood from
his arms and hands.

                  CONAN
       Its all theirs.

Conan looks himself over for a moment and spreads out his
arms.

                  CONAN
       A few scratches. Nothing serious --
       but that calf of yours needs to be
       looked at.

Olmec steps through the bloodbath and towards the two
mercenaries. His huge bull shoulders, neck and long, blue-
black beard stained with blood.

He stops before them, as tall as the Cimmerian but thicker,
breathing heavily, his eyes aflame and incoherent like a
campfire, his mind in ecstasy looking more like a giant
predator than a man.

                  OLMEC
       Twenty dead Xotalancas! Twenty red
       nails! If only one had survived so
       that I might skin him alive!
       Nevertheless, I am pleased -- more
       than pleased! The feud is ended!
       It is over!

Conan turns his attention to Valeria.

                  CONAN
       You'd better get that fixed. Let's
       have a look at it.

He takes her arm to turn her about but Valeria, the spirit of
battle still raging within her, throws off his arm.

                  VALERIA
         (agitated)
       Wait!
         (eyes Olmec)
       How do you know they're all dead?
         (to Conan)
       How can we be sure? This could
       have been a raid and no more.

Olmec, his mental state more or less back to normal, shakes his head.

> OLMEC
> They would not have assaulted the
> bronze door in halves -- it is not
> our way.

He sweeps a massive muscular arm to encompass the dead.

> OLMEC
> This was all of them. Yet, I did
> not realize their numbers were this
> low. Desperation drove them to
> this... it was their last attempt
> at victory -- only, how they
> managed to get inside of Tecuhltli
> is a mystery to --

> TASCELA (O.S.)
> -- By this.

They turn to see Tascela already near them. She stops before them, without so much as a scratch upon her beautiful figure, wipes the blood from the sword upon her lithe thigh and extends her other hand holding the pipes for all to see.

> TASCELA
> Behold, the pipes of madness. One
> of the warriors who responded to
> the alarm heard the last notes from
> these pipes, before the fall of
> Xatmec and Kametechol.

Valeria glances up at Conan who scowls and whose eyes narrow with disgust at the wizard's toy.

> TASCELA
> Tolkemec spoke of such pipes buried
> in the catacombs with the dead
> wizards, and it appears these dogs
> found it.

Conan considers Valeria for a moment and then looks from Tascela to Olmec.

> CONAN
> We need to make sure they're all
> dead. Have someone show me the way
> to Xotalanc, and I'll go.

Olmec looks at the survivors of the savage battle. Only twenty-one remain, including himself and Tascela.

Most suffer from minor if any injuries, but a few are on the
floor moaning.

                    OLMEC
          Who will lead Conan to Xotalanc?

Techotl limp-jogs towards them, his leg bleeding anew and
wearing a fresh slash across his rib cage.

                    TECHOTL
          I will.

                    CONAN
          The hell you will.
               (to Valeria)
          And neither will you. That leg of
          yours will soon be too stiff to do
          you or me any good.

                    YANATH
               (bandages slashed forearm)
          I will take him to Xotalanc.

                    OLMEC
               (nods)
          Good.
               (to another warrior)
          And you, Topal.

TOPAL, who sustained only minor wounds, is about to join the
Cimmerian when Olmec abruptly amends his orders.

                    OLMEC
          First help me and the others place
          the wounded on the couches so that
          they can be better attended to.

The Tecuhltli begin rounding up the wounded and carefully
laying them on the available couches in the Great Throne
Room.

As Topal and Olmec bend down to pick up an unconscious woman,
Conan watches as Olmec's beard brushes against the other's
ear as whispering words seem to flow from his lips, but
unsure, Conan scatters his misgivings with a shake of his
square-cut mane.

INT. TECUHLTLI - EAGLE'S TIER - HALL - NIGHT

Just past the threshold of the throne room entrance, Conan
glances back at the slaughterhouse.

Faces frozen in horrific, unfinished screams.

Intermingled bodies mixed like pretzels missing odds and ends covered in the eerie combination of the glittering green cat-eyes from above and the volcanic red-orange glow below.

A statuesque woman with a twisted mouth and wild eyes tries to pull out a dagger plunged deep into her chest.

Spilled bowels glisten in a pool of gore, eviscerated from a decapitated body.

A man with a crushed head, grips desperately to a broken sword while his other hand claws the air.

The remaining Tlazitlans move through the corpses, some still in a daze moving about as if lost.

He glances down at his torn and blood-soaked shirt and scowling at the loss, peels it off revealing huge rolling shoulders and a massive chest that taper down to a tight midsection.

His chest is covered lightly in hair and his abdominal muscles are chisel-cut.

Conan tosses the spoiled shirt into a corner and turns to rejoin his guides as together they move further away from the morbid scene behind them.

                    OLMEC (O.S.)
          You, Besala! See to her leg.

GREAT THRONE ROOM

Valeria limps after, BESALA, 20, into an adjoining chamber left of the dais.

INT. XUCHOTL - EAGLE'S WAY - NIGHT

A deathly silence pervades the air, meshed with the gleaming green and the unstable fiery light, as YANATH and Topal lead Conan surreptitiously past the great bronze door.

INT. TECUHLTLI - GREAT THRONE ROOM - CHAMBER - NIGHT

Valeria's left leg lies stretched out and unbooted upon a luxurious divan.

Feminine, dark hands work dextrously wrapping a linen bandage around Valeria's wounded calf.

Valeria watches Besala, annoyed and impatient at the woman's lingering manner in tending the wound.

Point down, her bloody sword rests against the couch near her sword arm.

A stream of blood runs down its length and mixes with the flaming floor.

                    VALERIA
               (demanding)
          Why go through the trouble to bring
          me here? You could have done this
          in the throne room.

Besala finishes tying off the wound and Valeria winces slightly at the pressure.

Still kneeling, the girl looks up at Valeria with limpid, emotionless dark eyes.

                    BESALA
          All the wounded will be taken to
          such chambers.

Valeria regards the calm disposition of the girl.

QUICK FLASHBACK - TECUHLTLI - GREAT THRONE ROOM - NIGHT

Besala viciously skewers a Xotalanc woman.

BACK TO PRESENT

Valeria's eyes leave the girl.

She pulls up her leg, examines the bandage around her calf and then stretches it back out.

                    BESALA
          Others will carry the dead into the
          catacombs before the spirits can
          leave their bodies and haunt the
          chambers and halls of Xuchotl.

                    VALERIA
          You believe this?

                    BESALA
               (nods; shivers)
          I once saw the spirit of Tolkemec
          in the catacombs as I hid by the
          tomb of an ancient queen.
               (MORE)

                    BESALA (CONT'D)
          His eyes burned in the dimness
          below and his beard and locks were
          long and white.

She inches a little closer and whispers.

                    BESALA
                    (apprehensive)
          Olmec laughs as do others. But as
          a child, I saw Tolkemec being
          tortured... and the spirit which I
          saw was him... older, but Tolkemec!
          They say that rats are to blame for
          the clean bones of the dead, but
          the spirits must have flesh as
          well. Who else could --

A shadow falls across the divan and their eyes dart towards
the chamber door.

Just inside the room stands Olmec minus his purple iridescent
robe, his massive, hairless dark-skinned body clean of blood.

Like a hungry hyena coming upon prime prey, his black eyes
devour Valeria's body while his huge fingers, assailed by an
occasional involuntary twitch, tug at his long, blue-black
beard.

Olmec steps aside and stares at the kneeling girl.

Understanding his silent command, Besala rises, bows and
heads for the door.

Past the entrance she turns a sideling glance at Valeria and
with a wicked smile scuttles away.

Olmec walks towards the divan and bends down to examine the
bandage.

                    OLMEC
          Not a bad job, but will it stay on?

                    VALERIA
          It feels tight enough.

                    OLMEC
          Put it to the test.

Olmec extends a hand to help her up but she waves it away.

                    VALERIA
                    (reluctantly)
          Very well, if you insist. But I've
          suffered worse than this.

As she places her hands on the couch and begins to slide her leg off, Olmec, in one quick, unexpected motion snatches her sword and tosses it into a corner of the chamber.

He scuds swiftly beside her and attempts to wrap her up in his massive arms.

But, Valeria, quick as thought, whips out the dagger from her right hip and jabs viciously for his bull-neck. But Olmec, though startled by her quickness, gets lucky and catches the deadly plunge barely an inch from his throat.

He smiles confident in his own strength and begins to twist her wrist until the dagger slips from her grasp and clatters on the pulsing red-orange floor.

Raging mad, Valeria tries her legs but he forces her down onto the couch by sheer weight and immobilizes them.

She chomps down on his wrist and draws blood.

Olmec cuffs her head with an open palm putting her in a daze.

Flashes of light suddenly materialize before her eyes and her head falls back onto the couch.

She blinks a few times.

Before her are three of Olmec and a room swimming all about her, before everything finally normalizes.

Her ocean-blue eyes burn at the gleaming dark ones and lascivious grin painted on his bestial face.

The fear of man, seizes her soul and reflects in her wild and troubled, beautiful eyes.

With wicked glee, Olmec rubs his brusque beard against her heaving cleavage, and Valeria cries out in fury and humiliation!

She pants and glares at him, caught in his web, but can do nothing against his mammoth strength.

Olmec lifts her in his iron arms and moves towards a door across from the one he entered.

INT. TECUHLTLI - EAGLE'S TIER - HALL - NIGHT

Much more like a thief than a prince, Olmec moves stealthily down a medium-sized hall with his stolen prize griped securely in his arms.

Though still filled with righteous indignation, Valeria does not offer any resistance.

She watches as Olmec pauses and listens for sounds of pursuit before continuing on tip-toes.

She notes his fear of discovery and screams for all the world to hear with all the power of her vigorous, sea-bred voice sending echoes bouncing off the walls and down both ends of the corridor in one last, desperate attempt to raise some form of aid and rescue.

Alarmed, an angry Olmec cuffs her again knocking her almost unconscious.

Quickly, he picks up his pace to a shuffling gait.

But the damage is done.

Looking back down the hall she makes out, through eyes blurred by tears and flashing lights, the form of a man limping after them.

She blinks her eyes for a clearer picture and is rewarded with the identity of the man -- Techotl!

                    TECHOTL
          Olmec!

Olmec wheels about and moves Valeria under one of his arms to await the oncomer.

Valeria renews her attempts to free herself, but her efforts are useless against the massive arm encircling her waistline.

Techotl stops before the growling prince.

                    TECHOTL
               (indignant)
          You dog! How could you do such a
          thing?! She is Conan's woman!
          They fought with us against the
          Xotalancas and you --

Bam! Olmec punches the poor wounded man to the floor.

He steps up next to unconscious man, stoops and takes Techotl's sword from its scabbard and thrusts it through his chest.

He casts the sword aside and repositions the girl in his arms and then looks back, with a leer upon his face, at the body of the man who dared contest the prince of Tecuhltli.

Olmec hurries away from the scene of his vile act until he gets to a spiral ivory staircase at the end of the corridor.

But unbeknownst to him and Valeria, another of his subjects witnesses his actions behind the cover of a hallway tapestry.

The woman watches until Olmec disappears down the winding staircase.

She then vanishes behind the tapestry.

From Techotl's chest the new wound oozes blood slowly.

Techotl stirs.

He awakens and groans in great agony and his hand instantly goes to his chest to cover the wound.

Techotl struggles to his feet and cries out in anger seeing what's been done to him.

His countenance is a mixture of sorrow and fury as his eyes begin to well up.

He looks down at his bloody chest while his hand strives to create a staunching seal -- and very light-headed and weak he staggers down the hall.

                    TECHOTL
          Conan! Conan! Conan!

The last drawn-out call for the Cimmerian echoes the desperation and despair of a wounded and languishing soul.

INT. TECUHLTLI - APE'S TIER - GUARDROOM

A door is kicked open and Olmec walks into a broad chamber.

All the doors are hidden by heavy tapestries except one.

A huge bronze door stands before them very similar to the one on the Eagle's Tier.

Olmec motions with his bearded chin towards the towering bronze door and gloats in a thundering voice.

                    OLMEC
          Behold! Another of the bronze
          doors of Tecuhltli! For fifty,
          bloody years they were guarded, but
          no more!

Valeria trembles in revulsion and outrage and her sapphire
eyes burn like hot furnaces.

> VALERIA
> You son of a whore! You'd still be
> sticking each other like pigs if it
> weren't for Conan and me. You
> bloody bastard let me go!

His eyes gorge themselves with her wondrous beauty, her milk-
white skin contrasting sharply against his dusky and heavily
muscled body.

The giant drops down onto a marble chair behind a chalcedony
table and Valeria writhes venomously as she lands on his lap.

She elbows him and starts kicking his shins with the back of
her heels -- one bare and one booted.

Olmec frowns and constricts her waist with a burly arm.

> OLMEC
> Behave, woman!

> VALERIA
> You worthless... son of a --

Valeria grimaces and grits her teeth in pain and quickly
complies.

> VALERIA
> (eyes narrowed; breathing
> heavily)
> When Conan learns of your
> treachery, he will gut you and cut
> off your head.

> OLMEC
> If I were you, I'd forget about
> Conan. Olmec, is lord here. The
> war is over. The time is now for
> feasting, drinking and --

He pulls her closer to his degenerate grin but Valeria turns
her face away.

Olmec is not deterred in the least, as with a wicked laugh he
licks her long neck with his fat tongue.

> VALERIA
> (detonates)
> You sow-ridden, crotch-stink! Get
> your filthy dog-face off me!

Olmec laughs, the laugh of an ogre, filling the room with his amusement.

His degenerate eyes alight on the golden vessel sitting on the table.

>   OLMEC
>   (reaches for the vessel)
>   Ah, this is what's needed! Perhaps
>   a little wine will help curb your
>   nasty temper, my love.

Olmec takes a draught and then puts it to her lips but Valeria turns her face away.

Olmec loses his patience.

>   OLMEC
>   Drink! Damn you, wench!

Olmec tries to force the vessel to her lips, but only succeeds in spilling the wine on her lap as she squirms to break-up his gross foreplay.

He attempts it again and wine splashes on her face, runs down her neck and between her cleavage as Valeria cries out like a caged lioness in helpless fury.

A calm, cold and malevolent voice sweeps into the room like an unwelcome breeze.

>   TASCELA (O.S.)
>   It is a very unbecoming to force
>   our lovely guest... an ally, to
>   drink wine against her will.

Olmec freezes. His dark eyes transform from lust to fear at the sound of the merciless voice.

He turns his confounded face towards Tascela, Valeria forgotten yet still trapped in his grasp.

Tascela stands tall and beautiful, before a tapestry concealing a door, with one hand hid behind the small of her back and the other fine hand resting tantalizingly on a shifted hip.

>   TASCELA
>   Not courtly in the least.
>   Especially for the prince of
>   Tecuhltli.

Olmec's dusky complexion takes on an ashen hue as he stares dumbfounded at the regal princess.

The princess brings forth a small golden cup from behind her back.

                    TASCELA
          (COOS)
      I knew she would not care for your
      wine, so I brought my own... the
      wine of old. From the shores of
      Lake Zuad.

Thick beads of sweat breakout on Olmec's forehead and his arm around Valeria's waist relaxes.

Feeling freedom, Valeria instantly slides off his lap and from his grasp moving quickly to the other side of the table to face the princess.

                    TASCELA
          (to Valeria)
      He remembers.

Though free from Olmec, Valeria's will is hampered by the burning, hypnotic eyes of Tascela and the reverberations of her deceptively soothing voice still sounding in her ears.

Unable to leave, Valeria can only watch in wonder.

Her straight, fine hair glistening in the eerie lights of Xuchotl, Tascela, with the golden cup held by both hands near her waistline, glides sinuously towards Olmec.

Her shapely hips swaying seductively. Her long, smooth legs beckoning.

Tascela's gentle, soothing tone, fills the room with a lover's voice.

                    TASCELA
      You sought to keep our beautiful
      guest to yourself knowing full
      well, that I too desired... to be
      her friend.

She glances at Valeria with a slight, sinister smile.

Valeria gulps involuntarily and her reckless eyes pale at the sight of Tascela's burning orbs -- inhuman and forboding.

Tascela places the golden cup on the table with one hand and with the other she fondles his long, blue-black beard with her long, slender fingers.

                    TASCELA
      Your ungenerous nature, vexes me!

For a blink in time, her veil drops and her face warps into a growling carnivorous beast, her eyes flashing as she rips a chunk of Olmec's beard from his face!

Valeria is left gaping by her sudden violence and unnatural strength.

Olmec jumps up bellowing like a bull! His angry roars fill the chamber with thunder.

Every muscle in his body seems to tighten like a trembling volcano about to erupt.

                    OLMEC
          Enough, whore! You, Stygian
          serpent! I will bear your insults
          no longer! This woman is mine! Be
          off devil-witch, before I send your
          foul soul into the hellfires where
          you belong!

Tascela throws a devilish, metallic laughter into his face along with the bloody strands of his missing beard.

Her mocking voice falls and flows like the soporific sighs of a whispering rivulet.

                    TASCELA
          Once, when you were young and your
          face was smooth, you wooed and
          loved me. And because of your love
          for me you dared sleep in my
          embrace beneath the intoxicating
          cloud of the black lotus. That
          night you became my slave. Your
          body, your mind, and your soul are
          mine!

She eases up against him and cuddles one side of her lovely face upon his chest as if it were a pillow, and closes her eyes.

Olmec stands powerless and listless before the princess, like clay in her hands.

Slowly, she brushes her face off his hairless chest and arrests his eyes with her powerful, burning gaze.

                    TASCELA
          The Stygian priest taught me well.
          All his knowledge of the black
          arts... all his secrets he gave to
          me. You cannot resist me...
                    (MORE)

                    TASCELA (CONT'D)
          you are my slave forever, Prince of
          Tecuhltli!

She presses close to him again and puts both beautiful hands
on his chest spreading out her fingers as she gazes into his
eyes.

Olmec's black eyes glass over and his arms hang loosely and
uselessly at his sides.

She twists towards the table with one side of her body, the
jewels of her circlet gleaming from the cat-eyes above, and
lifts the golden cup from the table and raises it up to
Olmec's dead lips with a wicked smile.

                    TASCELA
          Drink, my Prince.

Like an automaton he drinks.

The glaze over his eyes vanishes and a sting of panic wells
up within them marked by an unfathomable dread.

Olmec opens his mouth as if to cry out but cannot. His great
body lurches like a drunkard. His knees give out and he
collapses to the pulsating magma floor like a crushed tower.

Olmec's fall awakens the numbed senses of Valeria and she
dashes for the open door.

But faster than the eye can follow, like a blur, Tascela
materializes before Valeria blocking her escape.

Valeria throws a vicious, powerful punch straight for her
face with all the power of her lithesome body behind it; but,
with a pliant twist of her upper torso, Tascela evades the
blow and quicker than light she seizes the Aquilonian's wrist
before it can be retracted.

Tascela captures the other wrist just as quickly with her
other hand and then shackles both wrists in one hand and
drawing forth a leather cord from her girdle she easily
confines Valeria's wrists together.

The princess takes the cord and starts to lead Valeria
towards the table until she stubbornly resists.

Tascela looks over her shoulder and jerks the cord yanking
Valeria almost off her feet.

Once at the table, the sorceress motions for Valeria to sit
down and Tascela proceeds to tie Valeria's hands down between
her knees, to the chair.

After securing Valeria, Tascela rises and steps over Olmec's bulk and glides towards the bronze door, slides the bolt to one side and pulls the door open to reveal the corridor without.

As she walks back she talks to Valeria.

> TASCELA
> When we moved to Tecuhltli we
> brought all of our torturing
> devices with us... all except one.
> This one could not be moved and
> occupies one of the chambers in the
> hall. It's been some time since it
> was lasted used.

She stops when she gets to Olmec, looks down at him and with her handsome countenance, smiles fully upon him.

> TASCELA
> The time has come to stir it from
> its slumber.

An understanding fear grips Olmec's terrified eyes.

Tascela bends down and grabs him by the hair and lifts up his head easily to the height of her leg and seeming to know what's on Valeria's mind, she glances at her.

> TASCELA
> Oh, he's not dead. Far from it.
> He is only paralyzed for a short
> time. He can see, think... and,
> feel.

A low, gloating laughter passes through her lips as she drags the giant man along the floor as if he were a mere blanket.

Valeria is left bewildered at the woman's incredible strength as she drags Olmec down the hall and finally enters one of its chambers with the prince in tow.

Valeria battles in vain with the cord binding her to the seat as the clang of metal echoes down the hall and into the guardroom.

> VALERIA
> (in a subdued voice)
> Damn it!

Frustrated and desperate, she growls quickly and forcefully, her eyes flashing like a tigress caught in a trap.

INT. TECUHLTLI - APE'S TIER - GUARDROOM - LATER

Tascela enters casually, followed closely behind by a
groaning, muffled voice, closes the bronze door leaving it
unbolted -- shutting out Olmec's gagged groans -- and crosses
the floor towards her prisoner.

She grabs Valeria's thick, golden locks and pulls her head
back and inspects her coldly as she would a side of beef.

Valeria looks at the witch's burning orbs of fire, and
shivers.

Princess Tascela releases her hold and walks away for a few
steps as she speaks.

                    TASCELA
          You are highly favored, Valeria. I
          have bestowed a great honor upon
          you.
               (turns around)
          Your youthful vitality shall ensure
          my youth and beauty.

Valeria frowns and stares at the princess searching for signs
of madness.

Tascela, understanding, drops her chin and her dark eyes
follow the hands as they slide up from her thighs following
the curvature of her beautiful figure stopping underneath her
firm breasts.

She then extends her arms out to either side and shoots her
mesmerizing eyes at the Aquilonian blonde.

                    TASCELA
          Behold this body. Though young, it
          is very old. So old, that I cannot
          remember ever having been a child.

She clasps her hands together before her navel.

                    TASCELA
          In my youth I was loved by a
          Stygian priest and he gave me the
          secret of immortality -- youth
          forever!

Her eyes blaze like twin supernovas for a split second before
normalizing to dark pools of burning, hypnotic power.

Tascela considers Valeria with a dark smile.

                    TASCELA
          Soon after, he was poisoned... so
          they say. The palace he bequeathed
          me, became my home and there I
          lived for countless years by the
          shores of Lake Zuad... ageless,
          until one day the king of Stygia
          sought to make me his own. I was
          the cause of that rebellion of
          which Olmec spoke.

She drops her supple arms to her side and steps up before the
bound girl.

                    TASCELA
          Though called a princess, I am not
          of royal blood. Yet, no princess
          can compare to me and you will
          perpetuate my life, my youth and my
          beauty.

Tascela crouches and unbinds Valeria and has her rise to her
feet.

Valeria stands before the taller woman, helpless, her body
trembling slightly as her fear-ridden eyes are bored into by
the hypnotic, burning powers of the Tecuhltli witch!

INT. XUCHOTL - FOURTH FLOOR - CHAMBER - NIGHT

The two warriors lead Conan across a large chamber, elegantly
decorated with several tables, benches, divans, tapestries
and lush furs scattered throughout the pulsing tiles.

Once at the far wall, Yanath opens a door and in single file
they disappear from the chamber.

SERIES OF SHOTS - PATHWAYS TO XOTALANC

1) Yanath and Topal peep into chambers before entering
leading Conan through a familiar labyrinth.

2) Conan follows on their heels down narrow and wide
corridors only to once again enter a series of interconnected
rooms.

3) They emerge from a chamber into the Great Hall and as
they cross it towards the eastern side, Yanath and Topal draw
their swords and Conan is not slow to follow.

4) With brandished swords they traverse the chambers and
corridors they come to, even more warily than before.

5) They negotiate an ivory, spiral staircase up to the fourth floor and from there into a maze of more chambers.

6) Finally at the end of a long, broad, eerie-lit corridor they come face-to-face with the huge, Xotalanc bronze door.

INT. XUCHOTL - XOTALANC'S WAY - NIGHT

Conan tries the door and it opens without a sound. Behind him, the two uneasy Tecuhltli enter the enemy's camp, reluctantly.

INT. XUCHOTL - XOTALANC - FOURTH FLOOR - GUARDROOM - NIGHT

The heightened, nervous breathing of Yanath and Topal is the only sound discernable within the large, square guardroom.

Though different in regards to furnishings and the general arrangement of the items within, the Xotalanc fortress is an exact duplicate of the Tecuhltli fortress.

Conan puts away his sword and heads for an open door before them.

Once there, his guides a safe distance behind him, Conan looks down the hallway furnished by pillowed divans having high and very narrow marble tables on either side and garnished with fine tapestries, and exquisite rugs.

Conan, squints, as he scouts for movement or sound down the gauntlet of doorways.

At the far end of the passage he makes out the closed ornate, metal door that opens into the Great Throne Room.

                    CONAN
               (without looking back)
          Stay close.

Conan enters the long hallway.

Yanath and Topal hesitate.

Yanath gulps and sheathes his sword.

Topal takes a deep breath in an attempt to check his fast, fearful breathing and likewise puts away the sword.

INT. XOTALANC - FOURTH FLOOR - HALL - NIGHT

In single file they proceed down the hall, with Conan in the lead, Yanath behind him and Topal bringing up the rear.

Betrayed by a subtle, unfelt wind, the movement of a magnificent undulated hanging, draws Topal's attention. It billows silently outward and is then sucked inward, past the flush of the wall, into what appears to be a hollow behind it.

Topal pauses and takes hold of one side of the hanging and slowly slides it fully to one side like a curtain.

In a state of abject fear, his lips begin to tremble uncontrollably.

Conan, about a third of the way down the hallway, becomes inexplicably troubled, his wild, innate sense kicking-in.

He spins around.

                    CONAN
                (to self)
          What the hell?

Conan finds Yanath at hand and Topal stopped further back in a state of fascinated horror.

Topal's arms are up in front of his chest as if to ward off some fiend.

His eyes bulge, unblinkingly, in a state of unreasoning fear as they stare at something, apparently, beyond the wall.

Once beside the entranced man, Conan's puzzlement is replaced by disgust as his face cringes at the sight.

Coiled-up high in an alcove is a huge, strange, dead serpent, its head resting on top like a crown.

Large fangs protrude from the upper jaw down past the lower jaw in similar fashion to those of a saber-toothed tiger.

A huge, ugly gash lies open upon its neck.

Its only pair of legs, below and on either side of its huge crocodile-like head, are short and laced with daggers for claws.

Conan prunes his face at the foul reek as he notes its iridescent scaly, skin.

Yanath joins them and horror strikes him upon seeing the
coiled creature.

> YANATH
> (in a low fearful voice)
> The crawler!

> CONAN
> This must be the one I wounded on
> the stairs.

The odor is so offensive that the men move backwards until
their backs touch the opposite wall.

> CONAN
> It's strong though. Even with the
> cut I gave it, it followed us to
> the Eagle's Way... afterwards, it
> must have returned here to die --
> but how in blazes were they able to
> tame the creature?

Yanath breaks the spell of the saber-serpent to glance up at
the Cimmerian.

Yanath trembles and stumbles over a few words.

> YANATH
> In the catacombs there are many
> dark and strange powers known to
> the wizards of old, especially here
> below the Xotalanc fortress. But
> this beast, must have been brought
> from the dark tunnels below the
> catacombs... there lie the dormant
> things... dark creatures awaiting
> to be summoned.

> CONAN
> (mutters to self)
> I must have killed the last one, or
> they'd have brought another one
> when they attacked us.

Conan gives the rotting flesh one last look and moves out.

> CONAN
> Let's go.

Yanath and Topal stay close behind Conan as he pushes down
the hall towards the door at the end.

MOMENTS LATER

Conan places a hand on the door. But before pushing it open
he glances back at his two companions.

                    CONAN
          After we finish here, we'll search
          the rest of Xotalanc... including
          the tunnels, if we have to. I
          don't want any more surprises.

Conan shoves the door open.

INT. XOTALANC - GREAT THRONE ROOM - NIGHT

The wide throne room is the exact twin of the Tecuhltli
throne room. The same hangings and tapestries. The same
rugs and divans and ivory tables. And the same jade dais
mounted by the same ivory seat.

Conan is the first to see the morbid collection behind the
dais.

                    CONAN
          What the -- Crom!

Instead of a glistening ebony pillar stamped with countless
red nails, he sees rows upon rows of glass covered shelves
lined-up and stacked at intervals on the wall and encased
within them are hundreds of heads as if severed only
yesterday!

Dead glassy eyes looking at everything and at nothing.
Mouths open. Mouths closed. Bared teeth. Missing teeth.
But all having, except for the females, that characteristic
long, lank hair.

The other two finally discover the macabre exhibition and
follow Conan for a closer inspection.

Topal and Yanath, outrage and shock respectively playing on
their faces, stare at the heads of their brethren known and
unknown.

                    TOPAL
          Vile butchers! If any Xotalancas
          still live, their skins are mine!

Conan regards Yanath carefully as he sees the light of
madness begin to dance within his dark eyes.

Yanath eases up an arm and points a shaky finger.

                         YANATH
                    My brother's head!

He shifts his eyes and his trembling hand follows.

                         YANATH
                    And that, is my uncle.

He looks up at a higher row.

                         YANATH
                    And there is my sister's son,
                    Chototel!

With his eyes still glued on the staring heads, he begins to
wail, howling mournfully and loudly, his body shaking in the
throes of misery.

His tearless cries rise to a shrill, deafening pitch and like
a clap of sudden thunder morphs into maniacal laughter
followed by a crescendo of unadulterated screaming.

Yanath loses it!

Conan drops a hand on his shoulder, but like fuel on fire, it
releases the unreasoning, fiery madness within him.

Yanath, with one turning motion, whips out his sword and
slashes at the Cimmerian!

Conan jumps back in time to avoid the merciless cut yanking
out his sword in a blink of an eye.

Yanath's sword, now held by both hands, crashes down towards
Conan's face but Conan skillfully parries and as he does,
Topal charges the crazed man grabbing his sword arm.

Yanath, growling like an animal, foaming at the mouth and
flecking spittle before him, breaks free and rams his sword
through Topal's body.

Topal drops his arms to his side, his confused eyes staring
down at the blade in his body.

Yanath kicks the body off his blade and like a raging lunatic
starts slashing the glass shelves.

Shattered glass and heads fly ever which way.

Conan bounds towards the madman from the backside attempting
to stop him, but Yanath wheels about and lunges with a deadly
thrust forcing the Cimmerian to evade and maneuver out of its
path.

As Yanath pierces nothing but air, his momentum brings him past Conan and the black-maned giant cleaves the raving Tecuhltli diagonally to mid-chest.

Yanath falls dead next to Topal without a sound.

Conan takes a knee next to the mortally wounded Topal, placing his sword, close-at-hand, onto the glowing tiles.

Topal, gasping for air, is on the threshold of death.

Conan examines Topal's grievous wound, but does not try to stop the bleeding.

Conan traps the man's glazing eyes.

>   CONAN
>   (in a grim voice)
>   It's over. There's nothing I can
>   do. Any message, or last words?

Topal, eyes half-closed and gasping painfully, beckons the Cimmerian with a forefinger.

>   TOPAL
>   Closer... come closer.

Conan bends an ear to the dying man's lips.

Then instinctively like lightning, his hand, with a mind of its own, catches the wrist of a hand-gripped dagger meant for his side.

Conan, taken aback by the man's incomprehensible act, looks from the dagger to Topal.

>   CONAN
>   Crom!
>   (indicating Yanath)
>   Have you gone mad, like him?

>   TOPAL
>   As we lifted... the bodies to the
>   couches... Olmec ordered me to kill
>   you... on are way back to Tecuh --

Topal's head pivots slowly to one side and his vacant eyes stare at the dead corpse beside him.

Conan's features are a mixture of indignation and perplexity.

                    CONAN
              (shakes head; to self)
          They're insane. Every damn one of
          them.

Conan glances down at his dead companions, grabs the
broadsword and rises.

He stares at the undamaged trophy cases and turns away.

Long dead, glassy eyes follow him as he exits the throne
room.

SERIES OF SHOTS - BACK TO TECUHLTLI

1) Conan moves past the guardroom and bronze door and into
Xotalanc's Way.

2) Unerringly with sword in hand he makes his way through the
maze of chambers and halls.

3) He peers intently and cautiously into dark and shadowy
chambers, staircases, alcoves and niches.

4) He descends gingerly down a spiral staircase until he
reaches the bottom chamber.

INT. XUCHOTL - FIRST FLOOR - CHAMBER

As Conan steals across the floor, a labored breathing reaches
his keen ears. Agonizing, moaning gutturals follow faltering
movements.

INT. XUCHOTL - GREAT HALL - NIGHT

Conan emerges from a chamber on the eastern side of the Great
Hall and beholds a man dragging his body from the other side
clutching his chest.

The wounded man inches forward using one arm and his feet, a
trail of blood in his wake upon the pulsing, magma floor.

Conan recognizes him immediately and hastens towards him.

                    CONAN
          Techotl!

Techotl smiles weakly at Conan's alarmed face, and as the
Cimmerian kneels beside him, he rolls back into one of
Conan's powerful arms, unable to continue.

Blood spurts from his mouth as he tries to check a sudden coughing spell.

His face is soaked in sweat and his body shivers.

The hand pressed against his chest covers a ghastly wound but does nothing to staunch the flow of blood escaping between his fingers.

                    CONAN
               (through clinched jaws)
          Who did this to you?

                    TECHOTL
          Olmec -- he took Valeria! I stood
          against him --

Techotl grimaces, suffering greatly.

Conan's fierce eyes blaze.

                    TECHOTL
               (chokes a bit on blood)
          But as you can see... I was unable
          to stop him... he struck me down
          with his fist. The coward drove
          his blade into my chest... while I
          lay unconscious on the floor. May
          he burn in the hellfires of Stygia
          forever!

                    CONAN
               (more to self than to
                Techotl)
          No wonder that dog, Topal, tried to
          kill me!

                    TECHOTL
          He thought me dead, but I rose and
          walked until I was forced to crawl,
               (tears running from his
                eyes)
          in my own blood!

He stares down at the mess he's in and a surge of anger rises in him.

                    TECHOTL
          Watch for his treachery! He may
          have laid an ambush, foreseeing his
          plans undone. Kill the dog and
          flee!

A bloody coughing fit seizes him for a moment.

>   TECHOTL
>   Fear not the forest. Olmec did not
>   tell you the truth. The dragons
>   killed each other off... long ago.
>   The one you killed... was the last.
>   Olmec worshipped the dragon... he
>   sacrificed his own people to the
>   foul creature! Young and old. May
>   his carcass rot... with a thousand
>   devils!

Techotl, enervated by the sudden zeal, takes hold of Conan's
arm.

Tears of friendship well up in the unfortunate man's eyes.

>   TECHOTL
>   Conan, it was good to fight with
>   you... and Valeria -- hurry, Conan!
>   You must reach her before --

With blood still oozing from his mouth, Techotl's moist eyes
close as if falling asleep and his hold on the Cimmerian's
arm relaxes.

Conan gently places the lax arm on the wounded body and lays
Techotl down onto the fiery floor reverently.

Conan picks up his sword and rises slowly to his full height.
His eyes smoulder. His jaw muscles twitch and grind.

He shoots across the Great Hall parallel with Techotl's blood
trail without glancing at it and disappears into a chamber on
the western side.

INT. XUCHOTL - FIRST FLOOR - CHAMBER - STAIRCASE

Up the staircase he storms, rage twisting his face into
vengeance incarnate. As he rises higher up, smears of
crimson become droplets and streams of blood.

INT. XUCHOTL - EAGLE'S WAY - MUCH LATER

Conan emerges from a chamber still fired-up, looking like a
mad-hungry wolf on a blood trail.

He eases up from his dog-trot pace and coming to a complete
stop, drops the flat of the blade onto a huge shoulder.

He taps the broadsword on his shoulder as he curbs his
berserker rage and thinks.

                    CONAN
              (to self)
          Minus Topal, Yanath... and
          Techotl... that leaves eighteen
          dogs to kill!

Satisfied, he's about take off again when a recent memory
suddenly pulls his reigns.

                    TECHOTL (V.O.)
          Watch for his treachery! He may
          have laid an ambush.

Techotl's dead voice trails away.

                    CONAN
              (growls)
          Damn it!

His eyes dart up towards the skylights and a patch of
glimmering stars meet his frustrated gaze.

Conan moves ahead poking his head into several chambers until
he finds one with a staircase.

INT. XUCHOTL - FOURTH FLOOR - CHAMBER - STAIRCASE - NIGHT

Conan hustles down a spiral ivory staircase.

INT. XUCHOTL - THIRD FLOOR - CHAMBER - NIGHT

He steps off onto a landing and trots across the room and out
the door.

INT. XUCHOTL - APE'S WAY - CONTINUOUS

Through the rays of fire-stones, Conan with a naked sword,
moves swiftly but silently.

Far in the distance, at the end of the hall, he makes out the
great bronze door that leads into Tecuhltli.

Then an inescapable sound stops him like a wall suddenly
thrust before him.

He angles his thick, raven-black mane just a tab to one side
and again the sound is repeated coming from somewhere in
front of him.

He squints his eyes trying to pinpoint what sounds like a
struggling, muffled voice.

The intermittent sound leads Conan to an open doorway on the left.

INT. APE'S WAY/INT. TORTURE CHAMBER

An astonished Conan finds the prince of Tecuhltli laid out on an iron rack, as if on a bed, only several inches above the floor, gagged and bound.

His arms are pinned along his side. His legs are spread slightly apart. The wrists and ankles are wrapped by shackles that are integrated with the rack leaving no slack.

For a pillow, his head rests on a disk of spikes, already stained by his blood.

Above Olmec's huge, hairless chest hangs an enormous iron ball suspended from a circular opening in the ceiling by a chain.

Conan, leaning against the jamb of the doorway, watches Olmec who's still unaware of the Cimmerian's presence.

Suffering, Olmec grunts and grimaces and unable to withstand the pain of the spikes needling the back of his head, he raises it.

A lethargic clicking, clinking sound fills the deathly silent room and the massive iron ball begins to descend like a giant, heavy spider on a single, stubborn thread.

No cogs, gears, escapements or levers are visible. The ingenious mechanism, like that of a clock, is hidden from view.

Olmec's wide, fear-laden eyes watch the giant ball creep downwards towards his chest for only a moment before lowering his head back onto the disk and, with his bull-neck muscles, presses down against the hungry spikes.

The iron ball stops dead. Too ponderous for any movement to be detected, it hangs in the air like a grim and implacable executioner.

Olmec finally senses a presence and rolls his eyes delicately in Conan's direction. He grunts, his dark, desperate eyes pleading for succor, like a huge pig being dragged from the pen by its hind legs for slaughter.

Conan steps in.

INT. XUCHOTL - THIRD FLOOR - TORTURE CHAMBER

Conan stares down at the suffering man, a quizzical smile on his thin lips.

> CONAN
> Well, burn my leather if I'm not a
> Kushite!

Conan rests the point of his sword on the floor on his right side, the ever changing fiery hues of the tiles reflecting off the steel blade.

> CONAN
> How the hell did you end up like
> this?

Indiscernible words try to move past the gag in his mouth.

Conan extends his sword and surgically saws off the cloth strapped around Olmec's mouth and neck, and severs it.

Olmec spits and coughs out the gag, causing the ball to drop an inch or two before he painfully forces the spiked disc downwards again stopping the iron ball in mid-air.

> CONAN
> (looking at the iron ball)
> Looks heavy.

Conan taps it with his broadsword. The ball does move at all, in any direction. Conan nods, impressed.

> CONAN
> (looks back at Olmec)
> It's very heavy.

The cords on his neck strain against the pain and his desire to raise his head.

> OLMEC
> (pleads)
> Hurry, man! Before I tire and get
> crushed!

Conan drops into a jade chair.

Beside it is a small matching table with a golden vessel and several golden cups.

He lifts the vessel and swirls the contents around keeping his eyes on Olmec.

                    CONAN
          Why should I? You deserve this,
          and more. I'd like to sit here and
          watch you get squashed, but I've
          got more important things to do.
          Where's Valeria?

Conan stops swirling the vessel, peers inside and after
taking a quick sniff sets it back down on the table.

He focuses his grim, scarred countenance on the suffering
prince.

                    CONAN
          Where is she?

Olmec grunts and exhales forcefully, in effort and in pain,
and without daring to move his head keeps his eyes upon the
hanging mass above him.

                    OLMEC
          Release me first... and I will take
          you there myself.

                    CONAN
               (shakes head)
          First, you tell me where she is.

                    OLMEC
          No! How do I know you will keep
          your word?

Conan leans back and toys with the sword.

                    CONAN
          Very well, suit yourself. My word
          is as good as any king's seal.
          But, unlike you, I don't betray my
          allies or kill my men without good
          reason.

Conan glares at the hairless giant who gulps in a chestful of
air.

                    OLMEC
          Quick, man! We must hasten or she
          is lost! Loose me before it is too
          late!

                    CONAN
          I can wait. Anyway, I'll find her
          eventually and you'll be crushed.
          But since I hate to see you
          suffer....

Conan slowly stretches out his sword arm and places the tip
of the broadsword into Olmec's ear, with the ease and finesse
of a surgeon handling a scalpel.

He gives the sword a trifle push. Olmec stifles an
involuntary cry and blood begins to trickle from the inside
of his ear.

Olmec stubbornly grits his teeth.

                    CONAN
          That was just a push. Next, I'm
          going to ream your ear until you
          talk.

Conan pushes the tip of his sword into Olmec's ear again.

The will in Olmec's eyes melts.

                    OLMEC
               (speaking rapidly)
          Stop! Tascela -- it was Tascela
          who took her from me. She is the
          true ruler of Tecuhltli, not I.
          She took your woman for herself.

Conan, getting the wrong picture, scowls and empty-spits in
disgust to one side.

                    CONAN
          Why that filthy, degenerate --

                    OLMEC
          -- No, Conan! It is not that! It
          is far worse than you know.
          Tascela is ancient. She is
          hundreds of years old. She
          sacrifices young, handsome women to
          remain as she is... unchanging...
          always beautiful. But inside she
          is blacker than hell itself. It's
          this hunger of hers that has kept
          our numbers low. She will do the
          same to Valeria. Drain her of her
          vitality to renew her own.

Conan removes the sword from Olmec's ear and lays it across
his thighs.

                    CONAN
          I take it, the bronze door down the
          hall is locked?

                    OLMEC
                (relieved)
          Aye, and the others. But I know of
          another way into Tecuhltli.
          Besides me, only Tascela knows of
          this entrance. Release me and I
          will help you save Valeria.

Conan hesitates to release him as he considers Olmec's words.

Olmec notes it, thinking the worse.

                    OLMEC
          Even if you forced me to tell you
          where it is, it would do you no
          good, for only I can work the
          mechanism that unlocks the secret
          door. We have the advantage. She
          thinks you dead and me of little
          consequence. All we need do is
          catch her unaware, before she can
          use the power of her eyes on us. I
          should have killed her long ago,
          but since we needed each other, we
          allowed each other to live. But
          things have changed, and together
          we'll be able to prevail against
          her. Once the devil-witch is dead
          you and Valeria will be free to
          leave the city with all the
          treasure you can carry. This I
          pledge!

Conan sheaths his sword and stands up.

                    CONAN
          Where's the key to the shackles?

                    OLMEC
          In one of the cups.

Conan reaches for a cup.

                    OLMEC
          Wait! Before you unlock them you
          must first disable the mechanism.
          If you unlock the shackles before
          reversing the iron ball, it will
          come crashing down upon me.

                    CONAN
          Where?

Olmec, with his eyes, motions towards the far wall opposite
him.

> OLMEC
> Behind the tapestry is a small
> niche. On its base is a vertical
> iron handle. Pull it back until it
> locks. Then you may unlock the
> shackles.

Conan steps to the tapestry and yanks it off the wall
revealing an ornate wall niche made of a solid, grayish
marble and on its base a vertical, iron lever.

Conan grips it and pulls it back until it locks.

The metallic sounds of cogs, counterweights, and chains
clink, clank, and click within the chamber as the giant iron
ball is rapidly sucked up into the ceiling and the opening is
slowly covered by a heavy, displaced portion of the lapis
lazuli ceiling -- the only area of the ceiling not covered
with the brilliant fire-stones.

Conan moves to the table and searches the golden cups.

His face hovers above them until he finds the one.

He crouches down and unlocks one of the hand shackles.

Olmec squeezes and stretches out his fingers a few times to
restore circulation and strength.

Conan taps his arm with the key and Olmec takes it.

He grits his teeth as he lifts his head carefully off the
spikes and twisting to his other hand, goes to work.

MOMENTS LATER

Bottom up, the golden vessel is held high by a giant hand
with the sound of sloppy guzzling.

Olmec sets the vessel back on the table, refreshed, and wipes
his mouth with the palm of his other enormous hand.

He turns to face Conan, who waits patiently.

The two towering men are equal in height, but that's where
the similarities end.

Conan's massive shoulders are just as wide as the other's but
he has a clean-cut look, that the other lacks.

His amazing bronzed muscular development is headlined by the impressive arch of his sweeping chest ending in a ripped, hard waist.

Olmec, darker and heavier, has an ill-defined midsection and though remarkable for his size and brute strength, he projects an overall offensive appearance. Bestial and repellent.

The contrast between the two men is overwhelming.

>   CONAN
>   (barks)
>   Lead the way -- and stay in front
>   of me. Better to trust a jackal
>   than you.

Olmec, offended, tramps off towards the exit, his hand twitching involuntarily as he strokes his long, tangled blue-black beard.

INT. XUCHOTL - APE'S WAY

Olmec leads Conan in the direction of the bronze door.

>   OLMEC
>   (in a deep subdued voice)
>   ... I learned this secret only by
>   chance as I followed Tascela one
>   night and saw her use it to gain
>   entrance into Tecuhltli without
>   being seen... or so she thought.
>   To my knowledge, only she and I
>   know. She would have killed me
>   long ago, had she suspected that I
>   knew her secret.

They pass several chamber doors before entering another chamber on the left-hand side.

INT. XUCHOTL - APE'S WAY - CHAMBER

The chamber has the usual trappings. A lush, lonesome divan is pressed against a wall minus pillows. The floor is bare of any rug. Marble seats and tables with golden utensils are concentrated near the center of the room. Priceless solid and striped tapestries hang abreast of each other along the walls, except one.

Flush with the naked wall is small golden disk, until Olmec pushes it in.

A panel swings inwardly, silent as a hush, revealing within a winding, marble staircase.

                    OLMEC
          These stairs lead straight up to
          the tower and from there, other
          stairs lead down to different
          levels and chambers. The one to
          the far left will lead you to
          Valeria. Now go quickly, before
          Tascela has her way with her!

Conan motions with his sword towards the opening.

                    CONAN
          You first.

The prince gives him an indifferent look from underneath his eyebrows, shrugs his powerful shoulders and dropping his head enters the stairwell like a lumbering giant.

INT. XUCHOTL - SECRET STAIRWELL

A green shower of dusty light hangs in the stairwell as they ascend towards the tower.

Conan follows a few safe paces behind Olmec and after the first twist up the stairs, the secret panel closes silently behind them.

Conan pauses for a moment as his roving eyes stare up towards the very high ceiling.

The conglomerated fire-stones appear like a gleaming emerald star hanging high above, its radiating, misty rays filling the stairwell like a fantastic dream.

INT. XUCHOTL - TOWER - NIGHT

Olmec rises from the stairs to mount the floor of a large, circular, and domed tower, followed seconds later by Conan.

Conan sees for the first time actual windows framed in gold and made of the unbreakable crystal found in the skylights.

The windows are spread evenly around the alabaster marble walls of the tower. The craftsmanship is exquisite, but Olmec is blind to it as he plods on ahead towards the several descending staircases.

Conan takes a gander through one of them and finds the roof made-up of a motley of structures and shapes.

The oval and colossal roof of Xuchotl resembles a mountainous desert terrain populated by domes, steep ridges, towers and turrets. Giant black silhouettes outlined by the celestial night-lights.

He turns away in time to see Olmec's head disappear below the tower floor and trots after him.

INT. XUCHOTL - TOWER - STAIRS

With the light of fire-stones at his back, Conan drops down behind Olmec.

Only the light from the tower, sneaking its way in, helps to break up the darkness as they descend for several yards until it ends at the glowing mouth of a brilliant corridor.

INT. XUCHOTL - WINDING CORRIDOR

They enter into an intensely lighted corridor, its ceiling clustered with countless, brilliant fire-stones.

For a good distance they shuffle quickly through a corridor with more twists and turns than a desert sidewinder.

After one final turn and a straightaway they reach a steep flight of descending stairs and here Olmec halts.

Unbridled screams and shrieks wrapped with fear and outrage rise up from below shattering the quiet stillness, filling Conan with astonishment and fury.

Conan storms headlong down the steps, past Olmec, with vengeance burning on his scarred visage.

INT. XUCHOTL - STEEP STEPS

IN SLOW MOTION

After several steps, his innate prescience whips him around in time to receive one of Olmec's huge mallets on the side of the neck instead of a crushing deathblow to the head.

As Conan reels backwards from the sledgehammer, he lets go of his useless sword and snags one of Olmec's arms with a powerful grip taking him down the steps with him.

Down the steps they roll. A tangled mass of bodies, legs and arms.

As they tumble, Conan's steel fingers find Olmec's bullneck, the muscles in his sinewy forearm standing out like thick steel cables.

Near the bottom of the flight, a loud snap joins the fray and like two giant awkward boulders steamrolling down a mountain, they smash through an ivory-paneled door.

INT. TECUHLTLI - EAGLE'S TIER - GREAT THRONE ROOM - NIGHT

From the foot of the once hidden and now devastated entrance and slightly to the right of the throne, Conan rises amid dust and splinters, above Olmec's dead body.

He wipes the dust and blood from his low, wide brow, shakes his black mane like a lion after a battle and blinks into view the Great Throne Room.

Conan's charged, fiery eyes squeeze into narrow slits at the strange spectacle before him.

A mixed group of nine men and women are distracted for only moment, giving Conan and the body of their dead prince a cursory glance, before returning their entranced eyes to the exquisite figure squirming upon a sacrificial altar.

They kneel silently in a semi-circle a few feet from the black altar staring at an Aquilonian nymph with degenerate passions burning in their dark eyes.

Around the base of the altar are ten golden candlesticks holding black candles.

A heavy green smoke floats slowly upwards from each candle in spiraling columns to join together near the ceiling creating an arching cloud of smoke over the black altar.

Valeria lies stretched out on a glistening black altar, that is parallel and centered in front of the dais, held fast by four men.

Two, hold her arms stretched over her head at the head of the altar, which is to the left of the dais, and the other two hold her ankles at the foot of the altar.

She's dressed in a white tunic reaching down a few inches above the knees, her small waist accentuated by a slender, golden sash.

She struggles but to no avail. Her golden locks are disheveled and she lies helpless in their hold -- in jarring contrast to the ebon altar.

Tascela lounges on the ivory seat twisting and turning with bronze bowls of incense all around her.

Columns of incense, finger-like, swirl and spiral upwards, wrapping about her naked limbs like an orgy of lovers.

Tascela's eyes alight upon the Cimmerian.

Powerful, brazen, burning eyes that join her wild abandon in scandalous laughter.

Conan glares at the princess upon the throne, his eyes ablaze, his soul on fire.

> CONAN
> (seething)
> She-devil, whore!

Hellbent, Conan clenches his huge hands into steel fists and advances towards the mocking laughter.

As his right boot comes down, the pulsating tile drops several inches below the surface and two metal jaws shoot out swiftly from opposite sides trapping Conan's leg in their powerful iron teeth.

Conan stumbles and almost falls.

He clenches his jaws and ignores the pain and scowls down at his leg caught in the floor trap.

Blood begins to darken his leather boot around the wounds.

He growls in anger at his own rashness and searching for a way to extricate himself, Conan studies the floor quickly but finds nothing but strange symbols on the surface near the edges of the trap.

Tascela laughs all the more but her eyes do not.

> TASCELA
> As you can see I am well prepared,
> though your presence is most
> welcome. Yet, I am surprised that
> a warrior, such as you, can be so
> easily trapped.

Her eyes turn to Valeria, her lingering gaze hungrily devouring the outstretched beauty upon the altar.

> TASCELA
> But, when I look at her, I can
> understand your haste... and I am
> no longer surprised.
> (MORE)

                    TASCELA (CONT'D)
                 (turning to Conan)
          But she is mine, Conan! Watch and
          see what few on this earth have
          witnessed -- afterwards, I will
          decide what is to be done with you.

Conan instinctively goes for his sword but finds his scabbard
empty.

Like a snared wolf Conan snarls as he tries to pry apart the
two jaws deeply embedded in his leg.

IN SLOW MOTION

CONAN

glances at the altar.

VALERIA'S

lovely head rolls to one side, her dire, ocean-blue eyes
pleading silently for his help like a seized, beautiful
gazelle.

CONAN

roars at his helplessness, a flaming sword in his heart.

BACK TO NORMAL SPEED

Desperately, panting and breathing heavily, his muscles bulge
as he strains again with all his might to pry the jaws open,
but he cannot. He then tries to rip out his leg, but the
teeth are bone-deep.

Conan looks at his blood soaked hands and then raises his
eyes towards the lissom girl on the black altar. He growls
and redoubles his efforts to remove his leg from the infernal
contraption.

Tascela rises from the throne listlessly as if in a dream,
indifferent to the Cimmerian's raging efforts to extricate
himself.

Her dilated, cold, unblinking eyes survey the remnant of her
clan kneeled before the altar, some with bandaged limbs or
torsos.

Then as if stirred to life once more her pupils contract
somewhat into reason.

                    TASCELA
          Xamec, Zlanath and Tachic... where
          are they? Did I not command all to
          attend?

A pair of dark eyes shift from the altar and rise to fix
their gaze upon the princess.

                    TECUHLTLI MAN
          They were with us as we lay the
          dead in the catacombs. Why they
          are not here, I cannot --

A sudden, frightening recall fills him with consternation.

                    TECUHLTLI MAN
          Tolkemec! That is why they are not
          here! They have fallen to the
          ghost of Tolkemec!

Fleeting murmurs and an uncomfortable commotion begins to
spread among them as they look from one to another with
wondering fearful glances.

                    TASCELA
          Silence! Enough of this foolish
          talk. The ghost of Tolkemec is but
          a tale for the feeble minded. I
          will hear no more of it!

Tascela pulls a stiletto-like dagger from her jewelled belt
having a golden hilt and a thin silver blade.

Toying with it, Tascela glides down from the dais, the wispy
columns of incense clinging to her like tethers of smoke.

She stops alongside the black altar, her eyes burning like
two fiery gems from hell.

They sweep Valeria slowly from the tip of her toes to the
crown of her golden locks and then drop down to her eyes.

Conan stops trying to break free. Like two lit coals, his
eyes smoulder in his bronzed, scarred face. One side of his
thin lips snarls wolfishly as he watches the witch.

His labored breathing is the only sound in the chamber.

                    TASCELA
          You will make me young again,
          Aquilonian!
                    (MORE)

                         TASCELA (CONT'D)
                I will rest upon your bosom and
                with my lips over yours, I will
                drive this dagger slowly, oh so
                ever slowly, into the depths of
                your heart. When death takes hold,
                your life essence will escape your
                body and enter my own, revitalizing
                me... nourishing my body with
                everlasting youth and beauty!

Tascela chuckles softly and wickedly at Valeria's wasted
struggles in a cold, disdainful, metallic voice.

Tascela bores into her eyes with black pools of fire and
Valeria's movements cease.

Like a shrouding serpent, she bends over the pacified form of
marble loveliness, slowly closing the gap between their lips
as her chest begins to recline upon the pirate's generous
bosom.

The mystical smoke swirls through and about both women like
ghostly serpents.

Trapped in their hold, Valeria cannot close or turn away her
eyes from those of Tascela's. Eyes which grow larger and
deeper like two storming suns licking up waves of fire!

Meanwhile, the kneeling Tecuhltli watch with their breaths in
tow, oblivious to Conan's grunting and heavy breathing as he
desperately reignites his efforts to free himself from the
iron trap.

Their glazed eyes are glued to the altar in tense
anticipation as the cruel blade begins to rise.

Suddenly, out of nowhere and everywhere, a low horrifying
snickering seeps into the throne room like a creeping plague.

Those before the altar and those at the altar restraining
Valeria turn quickly towards the queer and forboding sound.

The bloodlust drains from their eyes, supplanted by abject
fear.

Tascela raises her simmering visage towards the source of the
interruption and lowering the blade to her side, rises from
Valeria's bosom, releasing the girl from bewitchment.

To the left of the black altar and within the frame of a
doorway stands a torn and tattered man -- more bone than
flesh -- held together by skin that is more reptilian than
human and by the very rags that clothe him.

A hoary shock of matted hair covers his head and from his gaunt inhuman face depends a beard of tangled confusion that reaches down to his skeletal chest.

Embedded in the man's ghoulish countenance are two unblinking eyes resembling a pair of blazing solitaires.

His mouth hangs half open and silent of any words. Only a shrill, cackling giggle streams forth from his age-old lips.

The intensity of Tascela's hellish eyes increases for a flickering moment, when she finally recognizes the snickering apparition.

>   TASCELA
>   (hisses)
>   Tolkemec!

She sways cautiously towards the head of the altar and stops tall and straight with her sleek back towards the two men restraining Valeria's arms.

The two men crane their heads around her for a better look, yet are resolved like the two others at the foot of the altar, in keeping the squirming Valeria in check.

The others hug closer together like petrified sheep.

>   TASCELA
>   So the tales are true, you live!
>   It explains my three missing
>   warriors... and many others.

Emotion, long dead, ignites her cold, beautiful face covering it with trepidation.

>   TASCELA
>   Why now? Why come up from among
>   the dead -- from the very ones you
>   feed upon?

Her deadly eyes narrow.

>   TASCELA
>   Ah, I see. You sought something.
>   What did you seek, Tolkemec? A
>   wizard's weapon? A weapon of
>   destruction... of power?

Tolkemec replies with a nerve shattering trilling snicker and leaps with unexpected agility over the hidden entrance floor-trap to land safely within the Great Throne Room.

Tascela shrinks backwards a step, sudden fear entering her
dark soul as she spies in Tolkemec's claw a precious wand
hewn from jade crystal and having a ruby stone on its tip.

                         TASCELA
                 (speaking more to self
                  than to Tolkemec)
            You have found a weapon! Revenge
            was your sustenance... more than
            the flesh of the dead. Twelve long
            years haunting through the darkness
            of the catacombs and tunnels... all
            for revenge.

A crooked slit splits his mouth exposing a full set of worn
teeth amounting to what could be misconstrued as a grin.

                         TASCELA
            No, you have not forgotten... have
            you?

TOLKEMEC

swiftly raises his dilapidated arm and points the unworldly
wand at the witch princess. The

RUBY STONE

blazes a brilliant red, drones like a squadron of dragonflies
and shoots out a red beam of fire.

Like quicksilver,

TASCELA

leaps to one side dodging the red blast of energy which
instead passes through the

BACK

of one of the men holding Valeria's hands, bursting from his
chest and striking the altar crackling like a mini
thunderstorm with blue flashes of light. The

MAN

transforms and crumbles into a pile of dust.

Pandemonium takes over the Great Throne Room as the black
metal altar is abandoned by the remaining three.

VALERIA

instantly rolls off the altar towards the dais and staying
low to the pulsing floor, crawls as quickly as she can to
Conan's side.

TOLKEMEC

with incredible agility, positions himself so as to trap a

FLEEING WARRIOR

between himself and a metal door. The

WAND

speaks and the

WARRIOR

explodes into ashes.

TWO

try for separate doors and their

CHESTS

burst open with energy blasts, which following through,
explode upon the

METAL DOORS

with blue flashes, as their

BODIES

fall into heaps of ashes.

MEN AND WOMEN

scream and fall over each other trying to evade

Tolkemec's wand

as he prances and leaps about the throne room like a
gamboling colt dealing death to all who get caught between
metal and wand. A

BRAVE WARRIOR

charges him with a brandished dagger but with a bronze door
behind him, the wand blazes ruby-red and he disintegrates. A

WOMAN

crosses between the deadly wand and the altar, the ruby
blazes, hums and she is instantly pulverized.

TASCELA

dashes out from behind the throne to retrieve a heavy dagger
near an ashen heap and scurries back to cover. Her dark,

FIERY EYES

rise above the ivory throne as she bides her time.

CONAN AND VALERIA

watch in wonder as the snickering

TOLKEMEC

leaps about flailing his arms like a living scarecrow
obliterating all that come between him, the doors, or the
altar.

With Tolkemec's attention riveted on another victim,

TASCELA

hightails it from behind the throne towards Conan and
Valeria.

As the last one, a

WOMAN

shrivels into ashes,

TASCELA

reaches the Cimmerian's other side.

Once there, she kneels beside him and rapidly and deftly her
fine, tapered fingers trace over three random designs upon
the floor near the edge of the trapdoor and immediately the
iron jaws release Conan's leg and the tile rises up, flush
with the rest of the floor, once more.

She slaps the hilt of the heavy dagger into his large,
powerful hand.

A little winded from her exertions, her beautiful, rounded
breasts rise and fall proportionately.

                    TASCELA
          Destroy him, Conan! I cannot! His
          magic is too powerful!

Oblivious to his wounds, Conan springs up, his fighting
spirit hungry for action.

He steps forward crouched like a lion.

Sensing danger, Tolkemec moves towards Conan on soft feet.
Warily. Cautiously.

His blazing eyes catch the gleam from Conan's blade and he
stops cold to further regard the giant Cimmerian.

Like two fighters, they gage each other.

Tolkemec begins to circle Conan endeavoring to maneuver him
between metal and wand and Conan, despite his height and
weight, moves like a cunning panther thwarting Tolkemec's
design.

The Aquilonian pirate and the Tecuhltli witch, look on.
Their matchless bodies tense. Their wide-eyes fearful.
Their breaths short. Their contrasting complexions wondrous
to behold.

The ghostly slide of Tolkemec and the quick shifting of the
Cimmerian's feet haunt the chamber with their silence.

Conan's smouldering blue-eyes are locked onto Tolkemec's
inhuman gaze, his grim, scarred face deadlier than hell.

Like a complicated chess game every move is countered and
counter-countered. Yet, while Tolkemec strives for
positioning, every step brings Conan closer to the wand-
wielding skeleton.

Tasting blood, Conan's body, legs and demeanor signal a
coming assault but his wide back crosses into the path
between a bronze door and Tolkemec's wand.

Valeria, quick to see, yells for her very life!

                    VALERIA
          The door, Conan!

IN SLOW MOTION

Conan hurls the dagger through the silent air and then twists
his body sideways.

The precious wand fires a red bolt of lightning.

The energy blast misses grazing Conan's abdomen by only
millimeters while the dagger rams hilt-deep into Tolkemec's
chest throwing him off his feet.

Tolkemec lands on his back, his arms outstretched, with the
dagger protruding from an emaciated chest and the wand, the
ruby gem gleaming, gripped in a bony hand.

With his mouth half open, the blazing eyes fade away into two
empty, dark sockets within the cadaverous skull.

BACK TO NORMAL SPEED

Tascela, her fiery eyes filled with power-lust, leaps up and
races towards the corpse of Tolkemec.

But close on her tail chases Valeria, her face and soul full
of fury and vengeance.

As she runs after Tascela, Valeria dips down and snaps up a
loose dagger among the heaps of ashes, barely losing any of
her momentum.

With Tascela only steps from reaching the wand, Valeria
springs forward into the air and drives the blade between
Tascela's shoulder blades with all the strength and power of
her arm!

Tascela screams in agony as she drops in her tracks one arm
still reaching out for the precious wand.

Valeria lands on the witch for a soft landing.

She stands next to her prey like a lioness and glares down on the dying features of Tascela.

Tascela -- her head to one side and her arm just shy of the wand -- pants rapidly, her eyes and mouth open in utter bewilderment, and as she dies so does the powerful burning light in her eyes.

Conan moves up stopping on the other side of the still body and glances down at the dead witch and then at Valeria.

Valeria doesn't look up at him. Her fierce eyes devour, with satisfaction, Tascela's death.

                    VALERIA
          Slut!

She looks up at the Cimmerian.

                    VALERIA
               (out of breath)
          I owed her that much, at least...
          for my self-respect!

Conan's eyes are calm as they face each other across Tascela's corpse.

Valeria's eyes drop down to Conan's bleeding leg.

                    VALERIA
          You need to be patched.

                    CONAN
          That's not what's bothering me.
          What I really want is food. I'm
          half starved!

Valeria grins as she plants her hands on her amazing hips admiring the Cimmerian's strong nature.

                    VALERIA
          I think we can do both.

She points towards the lounging area to a table topped with food and drink, surprisingly, undisturbed.

Once there Conan sits down on a divan.

Valeria begins ripping several strips from a hanging while

Conan removes the blood-stained boot and then stretches the leg out.

Valeria soaks one of the larger torn strips in one of the wine vessels.

After squeezing it a tab, she kneels beside him like a vestal virgin and cleans the teeth marks on both sides of the leg.

Conan's grim face doesn't register any pain or discomfort instead he watches intently as she begins to expertly and adroitly wrap up his leg.

After she finishes she looks up at his impressed faced.

> VALERIA
> I've had a great deal of practice.

> CONAN
> (grinning)
> That, I can believe.

Conan takes in her garb.

> VALERIA
> What?

While I admire the tunic and what it does for you, you're going to need a better outfit.

Valeria sees the light in his eyes and drops her eyes with a gentle half-smile playing on her full lips.

> VALERIA
> (looking up again)
> I can remedy that.

She stands up a little stiff from her wounded calf.

Conan pulls her back down beside him and without a word takes the still wine-soaked strip of cloth, wipes down her calf and taking a clean strip, applies the bandage.

Valeria watches as his big hands quickly and efficiently bandage her leg.

> CONAN
> (smiling slightly)
> Now you can go.

She rises with a grin on her lips and limps slightly towards the throne, the tunic failing miserably to hide her womanly charms.

Behind the throne and underneath the ivory seat she finds her shirt, her breeches, and a single soft leather boot mixed with royal robes and other paraphernalia.

With her clothes over one arm she throws the long boot over
one shoulder and heads towards the chamber where Besala
tended her wound.

As he puts his boot back on, Conan watches her swaggering
walk as her hips swing involuntarily, carrying her wondrous,
God-given curves into the chamber and out of his sight.

Conan gets up gingerly and tests his weight on the bandaged
leg and seeing that it gives him but little trouble makes his
way towards the splintered secret entrance. He enters it and
disappears.

The Great Throne Room is dead silent. Heaps of ashes with
scattered weapons and clothing are strewn throughout the
fiery, pulsating floor.

A witch and a wizard lie near each other in eternal oblivion.

INT. TECUHLTLI - GREAT THRONE ROOM - DAWN

Conan reenters holding his broadsword in his hand and as he
makes his way towards the lounging area his arm instinctively
sheathes the sword to his side.

Once at the lounging area he sits at the buffet table and
starts tearing away at the food.

He looks up at the skylights to be met by the first inkling
of daybreak, the stars barely discernable.

INT. TECUHLTLI - GREAT THRONE ROOM - DAWN (LATER)

With his mouth stuffed with food, Valeria walks out of the
chamber dressed and strapped with her two-edged sword and
dagger but with her boots dangling from one hand.

Purposely, she sits across from him on a jade couch plush
with white pillows of varying sizes and starts to slide the
boots onto her fine, long legs.

Conan stops eating and wipes his mouth with the back of his
hand and shakes his square-cut mane in amazement as he
watches her pull the boots up and over her beautiful, milk-
white legs.

She gets up and boldly meets his bewildered gaze and then
sits across from him on the table and pretending to ignore
him, she pours herself a cup of wine and begins to eat.

                         CONAN
              I'm glad I came after you.

She gazes up at him from under her lashes, stands up and walks around the table, giving her hips an extra umph.

She stops next to him and looks down at his upturned face with a beautiful smile.

                    VALERIA
               (in a hushed grateful
               whisper)
          So am I.

She, gently, catlike, runs her fingers through his black hair and clenching her fist in his thick mane, slowly pulls his head back just a little more and plants a long, slow and steady kiss on his lips.

Conan rises and wraps his huge arms around her back and small waist and lifting her off the floor, covers her with fierce, Cimmerian kisses.

EXT. XUCHOTL - MORNING

The gigantic northern door creaks open painfully.

Conan exits through the opening followed closely by Valeria.

Conan interlocks his fingers and stretches his arms in front of himself with gusto.

He glances down at Valeria with a zestful smile and then turns and scans the available view before them.

As he steps out, Valeria rests a hand on his upper arm stopping him in mid-stride.

                    CONAN
          What is it?

                    VALERIA
          The treasure.

                    CONAN
          Better to leave it. I want nothing
          from this accursed city.

                    VALERIA
               (nods pensively)
          You're right. Why chance it. We
          barely survived this hellhole.

                    CONAN
          We'll have treasure, soon enough.

EXT. PLAIN - MORNING

Behind them in the distance the sun hangs above Xuchotl as
they march towards the encircling forest.

Valeria glances up at him, the light of the day playing with
the blue of her eyes.

She then returns her attention towards the distant edge of
the forest.

She thinks out loud, annoyed.

> VALERIA
> It'll be months before we reach the
> damn coast... and I hate this
> walking.

> CONAN
> (grinning)
> There's no hiding it. You're a
> pirate to the blood. Don't worry
> though, I'll carry you all the way
> to the coast if I have too.

> VALERIA
> (chuckles)
> I don't think it'll come to that. I
> just don't feel right without a
> ship or a horse under me.

From a distance they continue to talk, the grim forest still
miles ahead of them.

> CONAN
> (optimistic)
> ... Anyway, by the time we reach
> the coast, the Stygian ports will
> be open for plundering.

> VALERIA
> (practical)
> We'll need a ship first... not to
> mention a crew.

> CONAN
> Just stick to me and we'll have all
> that and more.

LATER THAT MORNING

The edge of the forest looms before the two mercenaries.

Valeria's calm features change to apprehension at a sudden
troubling thought.

                    VALERIA
               (freezes in place)
          Wait a minute!

Conan stops and half turns to face her.

                    CONAN
          By Crom, what is it now, woman?

                    VALERIA
          How in Mitra's name are we getting
          past that forest?!

Vestiges of fear begin to creep back onto her lovely face.

                    VALERIA
          Have you forgotten, already?

Conan has no idea what's on her mind.

                    CONAN
          Forgotten what?
               (points)
          West is this way. If you're tired
          we can rest once we're out from
          under this sun. Come on... we'll
          be there soon enough.

Valeria does not budge.

                    VALERIA
          I'm not stepping one boot into that
          infested forest... not one!

                    CONAN
          What the hell is the matter with
          you?!

                    VALERIA
          The damn dragons! That's what!
          Remember?

Keeping a straight face Conan taps his temple with his
fingers and then slaps one of his huge biceps meaningfully.

                    CONAN
               (shaking head)
          They're no match for me. We'll get
          past them... even if I have to kill
          them all.

                    VALERIA
                 (snaps fingers)
          Just like that?

Conan pretends to ponder her mocking question.

                    CONAN
                 (nods slowly)
          More or less. I killed one... I
          can kill the rest. What choice do
          we have? We have to go through it.
          It's the only way out of this
          accursed place.

Doubtful, but realizing that he's right, Valeria yields to
his confidence and common sense.

She looks up at him, and nods.

                    CONAN
          Good, let's go.

Valeria gulps and scurries to the Cimmerian's side --
feminine and beautiful in her dread of the dragons.

Conan glances down at her from the corner of his eye and
struggles to maintain a carefree, nonchalant attitude.

She walks so close alongside him, that occasionally they rub-
up against each other.

EXT. FOREST - AN HOUR LATER

As they enter the sparse forest, Valeria unconsciously hugs
onto to him -- her fearful, beautiful eyes shifting and
searching.

EXT. PLAIN - SAME TIME

The sound of a shy, gentle wind stirs.

It whispers and lolls in place.

Only its sound is perceivable as it watches them a short
distance away.

Conan, with Valeria attached to him, slows down as they move
through the forest.

Then suddenly unable to continue the charade he bursts with
laughter.

Valeria is startled at first, then baffled thinking him gone
mad.

Valeria demands an explanation, but Conan in the throes of
laughter and slapping his thigh, cannot respond.

Annoyed she waits for his fit to pass.

Conan's laughter soon subsides enough for him to stand erect
but one look at her face and he loses it again.

Finally, the storm passes and Conan wipes his eyes, still
grinning and begins to explain.

Valeria's face changes from annoyance, to shock, and then to
anger.

She berates him but Conan grins and chuckles all the while.

Then boldly, the watching wind disturbs the sand below it as
it moves towards the two adventurers.

EXT. FOREST - MORNING

It troubles the branches and leaves and then Conan's mane and
Valeria's golden locks are rustled by its quick passage.

Conan, with one hand on the pommel of his sword and still
grinning, regards the feisty pirate with unfeigned
admiration.

Unexpectedly, he pulls her up by the waist, gives her a
passionate kiss and plants her back on the ground.

Valeria shoves his huge shoulder and, grinning like a big
kid, Conan taps her lightly on her backside.

                    VALERIA
          Eh!

Valeria playfully half-draws her sword.

                    VALERIA
          By Mitra, you're bold!

Holding his eyes, she resheaths her sword.

                    VALERIA
               (in a sultry voice)
          Careful, Cimmerian. You're
          treading dangerous ground.

Conan gives her a hungry look, fills his massive chest with air, and resumes the westerly trek.

Valeria puts an unsteady hand to her lips.

She watches as he marches off towards the thicker woods.

She moves her golden head to one side, takes a deep breath, her ample bosom rising, and exhales through pursed lips.

She hurries back to his side, glances up at him with a thoughtful, pleased light in her beautiful, ocean-blue eyes and then faces the forest.

Her left cheek swells as she tries not to grin.

Together, with slight limps in their gait, they push on, the dead city of Xuchotl watching them from far in the distance. It's empty battlements, great towers, turrets, and walls nothing more than parts of a gigantic mausoleum.

                              FADE TO RED.

The blood drains until the screen is immaculate white.

                         THE END